Up the Creek

Beverly Waters McBride

the Peppertree Press
Sarasota, Florida

Copyright © Beverly Waters McBride
All rights reserved. Published by the Peppertree Press, LLC.

the Peppertree Press and associated logos are trademarks of
the Peppertree Press, LLC.

No part of this publication may be reproduced,
stored in a retrieval system,
transmitted in any form or by any means,
electronic, mechanical, photocopying, recording, or otherwise,
without prior written permission of the publisher
and author/illustrator.

Design by: Elizabeth K. Peters

For information regarding permission,
Call 941-922-2662 or contact us at our website:
www.peppertreepublishing.com or write to:
the Peppertree Press, LLC.
Attention: Publisher
1269 First Street, Suite 7
Sarasota, Florida 34236

ISBN: 978-1-936343-74-4
Library of Congress Number: 2011923912
Printed in the U.S.A.
Printed March 2011

DEDICATION

*This book honors my dear mother,
Mary Louise Cato Waters, who left us this year
to rejoice with Creator. A good woman ...*

*My enduring appreciation rests with those
who make this possible and worthwhile:
Beth & Paul; Fae; Mike Menard, my inspiration;
Julie, Michele and Russ, chosen family;
Tom Poe, lifelong friend; so many Soo friends,
Julie from Peppertree, always supportive;
coworkers and my new fans;*

And, of course,

*BJ, my sidekick and protector;
book, box and grocery-carrier extraordinaire.*

Prologue

With my eyes closed tightly, I push up, up, up to the top, hearing only the sound of the wind rushing by my ears, my hair stringing behind me like long, happy streamers. I rise in the swing, straining for the top, still rising, rising, 'til everything slows down, then stops, for a only a second, as I reach the very highest. In that little moment, my breath holds, and my heart pounds in my eight-year-old chest, before I fall back, back, back and backwards. Remembering to breathe, through the middle of the swinging half-circle, my now curled up legs almost touch the ground, just missing the damp wood chips spread under the swing on the otherwise empty playground.

"Higher, Dan, higher!" I shout, hoping my new friend hears. My breath surges back into my filling lungs on the rise, up and up. I feel my friend Dan's playground-cold hands push on my back, just enough to send me soaring upwards again, faster. He is strong enough to send me up again, for this little while, there's only me and floating on air up to the top again. This must be what it is to feel free. But it only lasts a second or two, this nothingness between me and the clouds.

Then disappointment tugs at my tummy again, as the swing arcs back to where Dan catches up with me and pushes me up again. I don't have to ask him each time, he just does it. He's content to push—me, I'm content to fly. We swing, over and over. There is no other time or place.

"Dan, Mama says you come home for lunch right now," his sister, Melinda, shouts from across the playground. My eyes pop open, hearing Dan called home for lunch. The playground becomes real again, my swing slows. I sway to a stop.

"See ya' later, Beth. Don't go too high without me," he laughs, trotting home to eat, carefree, skipping, picking up and throwing smooth stones as he goes. He spins around in one spot and then runs to touch bushes and posts along the way. He doesn't look back at me this time, and his faded flannel shirt flaps behind him. He's a Native American, too, just like me, and also like me, he's a misfit. His hair needs cutting and his shoes are worn. But I like to see him smile a lot. He's looking back at me sometimes when I look at him. Actually, he looks at me a lot.

"Sure, see ya' later." I wave goodbye, still sitting in the swing, twisting, right, and then left on the strong chains above.

He runs home to his always busy house with people going in and out. The driveway and front yard look like a parking lot. Dan and his twin sister, Melinda, my new friends, are lucky to have each other, their big, noisy, family and their mom. It's fun at their house. They're twins.

No one makes me a bologna and cheese sandwich and a glass of Kool-Aid like they'll be having. No one will tease me over lunch and list out chores for the afternoon. I don't belong anywhere. No one calls me home. I don't have a family to run to.

I don't have anybody to talk to about anything. I wish I could talk to someone about these ideas in my head or show them my drawings. I see beautiful colors like dark green and purple and pink and yellow, and shapes, all jumbling together. I want to put them on paper, but I'm scared they're strange or bad. I don't know how to do things or I'd take care of myself without anyone's help. Someday I'll be able to take care of myself.

My tummy rumbles, wanting lunch, too. I should be grateful to have a roof, that's what I'm told, grateful that Great-Aunt El lets me live in her house and puts up with me. I am grateful—I am, really. But I want a real home with a mom and dad. I want more than a quiet house. I'm not sure exactly what else, just more than this. Aunt El is very nice, sure, but she's old and doesn't like me to touch anything in her house. Her glass figurines with lace doilies and plastic-covered furniture are not for play. I must be quiet at all times and not bother her. I'm going on nine now, and ought to be acting like a little lady, she says. I've heard the grown-ups whisper. If I act up, I'll have to go back downstate and live in "the foster care system." I know that wouldn't be good. Mostly I read and look out the windows and do puzzles in the spare room. The room I sleep in is not called my room, but the "spare" room.

Warm tears well up in my eyes again, as my head hangs down, but I'm glad to have these few minutes at least to soar.

 Chapter One

Washington & Maryland: Life as Mrs. Morrison

"Don't draw on everything, Beth," her guardian, Aunt El, admonished eight-year-old Beth. "Keep your mind on your studies. You need to stick to basics. Let go of foolishness."

She tried to conform, although thinking back now, some of her teachers probably assumed she wasn't too bright. When she first came to Maryville to live with elderly Aunt El, she played alone for long periods of time. She didn't possess drawing paper, didn't dare ask for any, but someone gave her crayons and a coloring book to keep her quiet, which turned out to be significant, for she took to coloring on everything. When pictures in the pre-printed children's coloring books were covered with her creativity, drawings far beyond the prescribed images on the page, she drew on the edges. She hid them, afraid of discovery, until Aunt

El found them, and thoughtlessly threw them out, considering them all used up and, therefore, trash.

As a young Native American girl, without parents nearby, expectations from others for her in education and career were underwhelming anyway. Her evolving theory was that as long as she didn't stand out, she would be left alone. She managed to keep those traitorous creative urges pretty much under wraps for years, so hardly anyone even knew about her artistic side.

Through all the "lean" years, art remained her silent salvation. Unaware at first, that the colors, shapes, and dimensions inside her head looked and felt different from those darting around in other people's heads, she learned that not everyone else needed to cover up their constantly evolving internal visual activity. She yearned just to fit in, to get by, reasoning that if no one else saw this same color and shapes business she constantly fought off, then she could keep hers at bay. Even a simple pastoral scene exploded for her into deeply saturated greens, blues, dark shadows and light trails, shapes and elongated curves. She never wanted to call attention or displeasure from others. Often she closed her eyes to clear her head to be able to move on, lest something mistakenly slip out to betray her. She learned the best antidote to the multi-colored, multi-dimensional images became to let them out onto paper, canvas, clay, or other available medium. Then she could keep only good ones.

Now, years later, as a young matron married to handsome dentist, Marc Morrison, her first priority revolved around social events, shopping, and other innocuous leisure pursuits. He swept her away from her adopted hometown, Maryville, Michigan to his home in Chevy Chase, Maryland, near the political and social hub of Washington, D.C.

Her job as wife and semi-socialite involved keeping Marc happy and trying, however difficult, to please his family. Naturally quiet and reflective, she still watched, observed and tried to fit in.

She suspected Marc tried too hard to climb up the D.C. social hierarchy. Once, she tried to bring it up, to suggest more meaningful commitments like a social cause, but he wouldn't hear of it. In fact, he became enraged, accusing her of criticizing and undermining him. She let it go and resolved to keep her opinion to herself. He believed a rigorous social schedule at fashionable events and membership in the "right" clubs was his ticket to acceptance.

Yet, despite his free-flowing spending and relentless socializing, as far as she could see, his progress remained pretty slow on that front. Sure, he laughed boisterously at parties with cronies, sailed grand yachts, toasted and roasted with politicos at thousand-dollar-a-plate fundraisers, yet real respect or regard eluded him.

The frantic social whirl she didn't enjoy so much. He'd inexplicably allowed her to enroll in college, provided it didn't interfere with his schedule of social obligations. He evidently accrued something from her taking classes, for he surely never allowed her anything without expecting something in return.

First married, as lovers, they talked for hours. Interested in everything she said or thought, he flattered her. They met while he worked as a dentist for the Tribe in Maryville. An attractive man, slim, almost delicate, he made sure to imply to everyone that he was 'somebody' and showed her the best side of himself.

She worked in reception for the Casino Hotel and also filled in at the Casino Lounge on busy nights. At first, he enchanted her with attention and lavish gifts, eager to cultivate her. He hung on every her word, indulged her every whim. They enjoyed dining out and going to cultural events, like the symphony and local theatre. They laughed at the same jokes, discussed and agreed upon everything from politics to movies, sports to music. He mesmerized her, implying financial security and a sparkling future of social acceptance. Both of those prospects sounded attractive, especially coming from her background, having grown up with neither. She had prior relationships, especially with her old love, Dan Walkin. He'd never been ready to commit to her. Instead, Mark emerged like a shining prince, easy to please and very cosmopolitan.

She, in turn, very much enjoyed pleasing him. He courted her in earnest, then asked her to marry him as if only the promise of a lifetime with her fulfilled his deepest wish. Eventually, she stopped working the lounge. Once engaged, she quit her hotel job, too. They married in a lavish storybook wedding at the Catholic Church in Maryville. There were times she regretted lording her good fortune over her friends back home, but she could spare no regret to think of that now.

Soon after they married, he petulantly wanted to return to his family home in Maryland, away from her beloved UP. She reluctantly agreed, loath to leave her home, yet optimistic about living with him in a new environment, a big, glamorous city they would explore together. She considered close family crucial, looked forward to meeting his family and sharing their affection.

As soon as he moved her out of her environment and she became dependent on him, he changed. He seemed to be under a malevolent family spell and she lived at their mercy. Suddenly, he found fault with everything about her and began to treat her more like some flawed "decoration" in his world of aspiring social connections and mid-level power junkies.

She knew Marc was his mother's pride and joy. Her son performed no wrong in dowager Mrs. Morrison's judgmental eye, except perhaps to marry her. Not from their "set," they often reminded her she'd been imposed on them from the wilds of the North. From their first meeting, Mother Morrison found fault with her and voiced it frequently. Beth still clung to the idea that whatever about her drew him to want to marry her, whatever tiny, lingering, redeeming quality, remained deep in her somewhere.

Why did he marry her? Was he so influenced by his family that he could be so easily swayed against her? Was bringing her here his lone act of rebellion gone wrong? She'd asked herself these questions before, yet never voiced them, pretty sure even a civil answer would be hard to get from him.

At school, her days were a completely changed milieu. While attending day classes at American University in D.C., she circulated in a progressive, relatively unrestrained environment. She sought her creative voice in art, art history and art education classes, her days at school yielding expression of long repressed freedom and passion. She excelled, collecting recognition for her work, honors she felt best left at school. She gave up pursuing several opportunities, as nights at home became oppressive and dark. At times, neither place seemed real, for even at school, she felt pressed to remain ever vigilant, wary and guarded, in case some social infraction leaked back to Marc. Consequences at home could be harsh.

Her favorite professor at American University, Dr. Bizant, frequently pushed her for more expression and detail, more color and more emotions. Prof held no idea of her life at home with Marc.

"More, more, more!" she protested during one of their lessons. She stood in her painting smock, hair seeping out from her unpretentious scrunchie, paint-flecked hand on her stuck-out hip. "I don't know if more is in there!" she objected crabbily.

"Remember, Beth, art is long, life is short. You rob yourself of the gift of expression by doing it only halfway," Dr. Bizant chided, drawing her eyes back into her barely begun masterpiece-in-the-making.

"But, Prof, it takes everything out of me. I'm exhausted," she whined plaintively, blocking out admitting, even to herself, the pain and anguish going on in her life elsewhere.

"Precisely. You want to get the anger, sadness, and regret out of there. I see in you something going on, something tragic and limiting. You owe it to yourself to express it." He'd pushed on her forehead with the palm of his paint-stained hand, as if he might shove good things into her head. "Make some room in there for joy and exhilaration yet to come. I don't want you to settle for half-measure, not in this arena."

"If you say so, Dr. Bizant," she shrugged, searching for her artistic muse, contending against her broken, hurting heart.

Chapter Two

One Dark Night

"Where have you been? Why aren't you ready?" Marc quizzed her, standing rigidly, red-faced, fists clinched at his sides. She had breezed in from school late one afternoon, with only a few minutes to transform into a quiet, dutiful wife and daughter-in-law.

"You told me you wanted me to be out from underfoot so I spent the day in town. Traffic was very heavy coming back this afternoon," she replied as she stepped out of a quick shower, donned her already laid out evening wear and scurried for her shoes.

"You remain determined to spite me, don't you?" His raged amped up, spittle collecting on the edges of his mouth. "I should never have brought you here! You subsist full of insolence and excuses. You selfishly expect the rest of us to wait on you or ignore your colossal rudeness. Perhaps you need discipline, just like a child. Tomorrow, we'll see you deprived of some of your privileges and punished.

Then we'll see if you manage to be ready when you're told."

Beth stopped her speed dressing. He practically foamed at the mouth. This time, he crossed the line. She looked at him with narrowed eyes, pride and resistance creeping over her face.

He slapped her, hard, leaving the hot, red prints of his fingers on her cheek. He'd slapped her before, twisted her arms, pulled her hair and pinched her, but never before hit her directly on the face just as they readied to go out. Shocked, she turned, picked up her evening bag, and exited with all the dignity she could muster. Walking down the plush carpeted hallway in the palatial home toward the formal curved staircase leading to the foyer, her step remained firm, her head held high.

Leaving him behind, she slowed to glimpse herself in the massive hallway mirror. Although Marc insisted on shopping with her, dictating her selections, she still managed to pull pieces together according to her own tastes. She wore a stylish, ice-blue, strapless satin gown, fitted to show her figure and trim waist. The dress flared elegantly over her womanly-rounded hips to touch the tops of her pale blue evening slippers. She chose simple, elegant, blue topaz earrings, with a stunningly beautiful blue topaz necklace, her favorite. Beth loved the single circle of faceted, flower-petal-shaped blue gemstones surrounding diamond centers that adorned her neckline. Small silver combs gleamed in the light, holding back her dark hair. Her small blue evening clutch sparkled with opalescent sequins and crystals.

She sensed rather than saw Marc behind her, hurrying past her on the stairs, as if to childishly reach the drawing room before her. Still on the stairs, she heard his whining voice poised at his mother's ear. The venerable Mrs. Morrison sat stiffly on the beautiful uncomfortable settee, an untouched sherry at her side. The elder Mrs. Morrison favored vintage Channel designs, this one in a pale pink, not a good color for her already sallow complexion—evidently, no one ever told her. Her less-than-flattering dress, topped off with out-of-style, puffed up hair, ostentatious jewelry and overdone make up gave her a bizarre look. She also wore sturdy footwear. Beth speculated wordlessly behind her hand whether Mother Morrison anticipated she might be hiking at this event tonight. Her husband, the stiff-necked, silent Mr. Benton Morrison, stood near the fireplace, working at ignoring all of them. Marc and his father wore conservative tuxedos with crisp white shirts, the prescribed attire for these events. They never considered deviating from the uniform.

They all looked up at her as she stiffly stood in the doorway. Each of them wore a different expression: Marc, triumphant since he arrived first; his father, indifferent; and Mrs. Morrison, disapproving. Beth wondered if her darkly malicious mother-in-law ever saw herself in the mirror, with her sadly wrinkled face—despite a fortune spent in spas—and drawn on, arched, black eyebrows framing her usual vinegary expression.

The room always reminded Beth of a reproduction of some modern decorator's high-priced version of a gloomy, foreboding Victorian sitting room: heavy, dark-wood furniture, upholstered with thick brocades, dull carpet and heavy, floor-puddle brocade draperies covering huge windows. The Morrison's evidently didn't enjoy illumination. Neither the room nor atmosphere welcomed guests, much like its occupants this evening.

"She provoked me, deliberately, Mother."

Her mother-in-law looked up, taking in Beth's still reddened cheek with a sour expression. "I only hope she learned a lesson here. A quarrelsome wife reaps her comeuppance. By the way, those slippers are not at all appropriate," Mother Morrison criticized self-righteously, flicking imaginary lint from her sleeve. "You should be wearing shoes for walking, not for the bedroom," she scolded. "It's too late to change now, you've already made us late, so you must go ahead."

"Don't worry, Mother, she'll be reminded tomorrow that her insolence will not be tolerated." Marc glowered toward her. Even more frightening to her, a calculating gleam emanated from his eyes. Was he enjoying this? It occurred to her this signaled a further escalation of violence toward her, which she previously persistently denied. Beth self-consciously curled her toes inside her graceful slippers.

"How is it you never manage to make yourself presentable for these affairs?" Marc looked her over, on a roll now for the benefit of his adoring mother, his contempt for her showing all over his arrogant expression and sharp tone of voice. "You remain a constant embarrassment to me and to the family." She looked at him, puzzled. He had berated her many times in the past with his parents present; however, he never before went this far.

Marc's father motioned them toward the limo for the ride to Embassy Row. Marc forcefully grabbed her elbow, roughly tugging her to the waiting car.

The three of them sat in the limo across from her, two glaring at her, with one ignoring her. None of them offered her a shred of approval—certainly no compliments, no acknowledgment of the hours of planning her outfit, or the taste of her choices. She only heard the numerous ways she failed to meet their standards yet again. She tried to change whatever they found objectionable each time they derided her, then a different complaint surfaced. They'd already pretty much decimated her outward appearance, before starting in on more subtle shortcomings, like her speech or her demeanor. After that, they went after her upbringing, her heritage, and even her youth. It hardly mattered anymore. Nothing about her suited them.

Marc's father straightened his formal jacket, then ran a finger inside his starched collar. He stared forward out the darkened window, as if tuning out yet another boring recital of Beth's failings. Once, she considered he might be secretly sympathetic, but he never intervened. Sometimes, she silently begged him with her eyes, blinking back welled-up tears. Still, he remained indifferent. Tonight, self-conscious about her "wrong" shoes and the poor impression they expected her to make at this dignified party with important, consequential people, she knew from past experience, the criticism she endured would continue and follow her home later that evening.

Looking for respite, she turned to watch the verdant Maryland countryside flying by along the highway. Beth enjoyed seeing urban farms give way to more densely populated neighborhoods, where lawns eventually turned huge again, with urban traffic winding around high-columned porticos on large homes. Sprawling lawns with flawless landscaping and curved driveways littered with sleek cars looked busy, as if every home hosted a party with happy people.

This social whirl existence ought to make her feel in on the beautiful life. She enjoyed everything that should make her happy—beautiful designer gowns, expensive fragrances, and all the shoes she wanted. She wore lovely jewelry, choosing simple, quality pieces, more to her stylized tastes than more garish pieces favored by Marc's mother.

However, her dreams revolved around security, rather than material possessions.

Although almost ready to admit that Marc no longer wanted to protect her or build a peaceful life with her, she still found herself wanting to please him. She clung to fantasies of a happy home to come up with what she needed to entice him to love her, to respect her again. Lately however, as her world became smaller, she just wanted to make it through the day and then the night.

"See what I must endure constantly, Mother? His face assumed a demonic twist, scaring her with the intensity of cruelty in his eye.

"Yes, I see perfectly, Marc," Mother Morrison almost spat out, her nose curled as if smelling something vile. "Yet again, it is beyond me how you ever imagined this, this …" she stammered, gesturing with splayed hands and long fingernails, "… person could fit in here with us." Beth wanted to tell them, "Hey, I'm right here," but let it go. Her mother-in law's expressions and gestures reminded her of the evil witch in Sleeping Beauty, only lacking the demonic laugh. Except Mother Morrison lived as no two-dimensional animated character and she herself no sleeping beauty.

"Do you understand your behaviors must not embarrass us tonight, Beth?" He warned her again, as his mother looked on, almost giddy with the censure of her errant daughter-in-law.

Beth tried to return their glare, but she caved first and turned her head to the side window, muttering, "Yes. I understand." Sometimes, like now, it just seemed easier to go along with them. She silently raised her fist to her mouth as if to stuff back all the replies she wanted to make. She kept her head turned away, hoping to deny them the satisfaction of seeing her tears.

"Oh, don't be so tiresome, please? Your tears only make you look silly. They don't sway anyone," Marc continued, like a shark sensing blood in the water. "You exasperate me so, I can't imagine what must be resolved so you finally realize how your behavior affects me, affects all of us. Right, Mother?"

"She has only been a disappointment to us from the beginning," Mother Morrison spat out. "Everyone in our set is aware of her deficits, believe me. They think she is inappropriate for you, my dear." With that, his adoring mother sighed, patted the back of his hand, 'accidentally' kicking Beth painfully on the shin with her heavy shoe. She glared anew, as if Beth ought to apologize to her for having the temerity to allow her leg to get in the way of her wildly swinging foot inside the cramped space. Beth knew she'd suffer a bruise on her shin tomorrow to remember this particular session.

After a stark silence, Marc and his mother engaged each other in gossip about who could be expected at this particular party. The banal chitchat served to draw their focus away from her for a while. They spoke venomously about a certain social maven, a politician's wife they knew rumored to behave scandalously. Her tears subsided, breathing returned to normal. Still, her heart and her shin ached.

Arriving at the party, the valet opened their limo door under the elaborate portico. They poured out like slow syrup from a bottle, taking their time, as if much too sophisticated to show any excitement over the coming social event.

Inside, they exchanged perfunctory platitudes with their hosts, and then Marc and his parents disappeared into the crowd. He never wanted her near him at these parties, since he gathered with his crude cronies to smoke cigars and ogle women. Beth suffered, lost, unsure, afraid to act or say anything, not knowing who among them might be critical of her or ready to rat her out to the Morrisons if her manners came into question.

She usually spent party time exploring the home, hall or hotel, observing the décor in detail and silently critiquing the furnishings and artwork. She loved going to historic Kennedy Center, or to an embassy ballroom. She loved to listen unobtrusively to conversations from small groups and enjoyed the exotic, international flavor that swathed these events. Their talk intrigued her, although she wouldn't dare engage in them herself. She circulated, always on the periphery, not joining in.

People of all descriptions arrived, becoming absorbed into the crowd. She heard several languages, French, German and maybe Russian spoken all around her—a typical gathering of Washington's social elite, politicos, diplomats, advocates, bankers, and social climbers. They dressed in stylish evening attire of severe black tuxes and pricy black evening dresses, with only an occasional brightly colored red or white gown punctuating the room. She stood out, without meaning to, in her feminine light blue gown.

People milled, regrouped, selected drinks and hors d'oeuvres from the trays offered. She stopped to admire a particularly interesting painting, looked closely to see if she recognized the signature, her head tilted to gaze further into the work, absorbed.

Suddenly, a jolt from behind bumped into her, causing her to spill a few drops of white wine from the glass she clutched. Instantly apologetic, she spun around. There stood a beautiful woman of color, resplendent in bright yellow and green floral native dress. Her mouth set in a round "oh," a horrified expression on her face. The woman had flawlessly smooth skin the color of milk chocolate, full lips proportioned to her intriguing face, with dark eyes shaped like almonds sparkling in concern. She repeatedly offered apologies in slightly British-accented English.

"I am so sorry," she said, gently touching Beth's arm. "I was not looking. I hope I haven't ruined your beautiful dress," the woman offered contritely.

Beth's hand grazed over the blue topaz necklace at her neck, unsure how to respond. She liked this woman instantly, one of those rare moments of immediate bonding. In a split second, she saw a possibility for developing an acquaintance with this attractive, polite woman. Timidly, she loosened up enough to speak to her.

"No. No harm done. I was just surprised." Beth's eyes darted around, looking for her husband or in-laws, in case they descend on her, berating her again. She prepared to move on, out of the limelight. She would be embarrassed for this woman to hear a recitation of her flaws.

"Let's go out on the terrace to talk, shall we?" She gently surrounded Beth's elbow with her warm hand, pulling her out of the room. Together they sauntered around the crush of people in the room through the great glass doors to the patio.

"Hello, my name is Beth," she said, extending her hand formally. "And yours?" She said.

"My name is actually long and difficult in my native language. Here, I'm going to be called Charlotte. Please, I am honored if you would call me by that name."

Silent servants ushered them to chairs at one of the small, outdoor tables and fresh drinks materialized. Charlotte leaned toward her earnestly, as if to hear

Beth's every utterance. Beth flushed, flattered to be the momentary focus of this interesting person. Colorful cloth, the same as the multi-colored ethnic garb she wore, enfolded Charlotte's long, dark hair. A fringe of perfectly curled lashes framed Charlotte's expressive eyes. She wore exquisite make up, especially round her eyes. Huge gold cuff bracelets adorned each wrist and long golden dangles hung from her ears, bold jewelry perfectly complementing her exotic dress. Ample may be a good description of her shape, although hard to discern from the looseness of the dress. Charlotte introduced the solicitous and solemnly serious man who sauntered to her side as Eddie, her husband. They all shook hands. Eddie gave her a courteous bow in greeting, flashed an engaging white-toothed grin and then disappeared, leaving the two ladies to talk.

"Eddie takes good care of you, Charlotte," Beth observed, a little jealousy rearing, contrasting her own situation. Envy was tamped down inside, along with her other emotions.

"In every way, my dear," Charlotte whispered confidentially, giggling behind her hand, eyes sparkling. "I'm a very lucky woman, no doubt. He wants me to make some friends here, to go my own way so I'll stay out of his hair, you know?"

Beth nodded her understanding, conspiratorially grinning back at her. Talking about something normal pleased her.

"Your English is excellent, Charlotte. Please forgive me, but I don't know a lot about your native country."

"Don't worry, my dear, I'll probably carry on about it quite soon enough. You'll probably eventually know more than you ever wanted to know. Actually," she continued, "I went to college in Tennessee at a conservative religious school, close to Ashville, so I picked up American language and customs. It's nice to come back to America, to be able to help Eddie. He studied in England and then returned home. He's a real stitch, sometimes, messing up on the idiom. Luckily, he's charmed by American idiosyncrasies. We married recently," she confided, "so pretty much everything's new and exciting to us. Now we're here in the U.S., at least for a while." Beth heard a note of regret in her explanation, as if there may be more to that story. She'd look forward to hearing it.

"Newlyweds, eh?" Beth joked, as Charlotte squirmed, unpretentiously covered her mouth with one hand and waved the conversation on with the other.

"Tell me about you," Charlotte said, at last leaning back, settling in as if eager to hear her story.

Enchanted by her newfound confidant, Beth animatedly opened up to her, recounting the surface of her marriage, discretely leaving out the hurt and humiliation part. "I'm from Michigan. Do you know about Michigan? It's the state shaped like a mitten with the fish above it." Beth paused, waiting for Charlotte to grasp her reference. Charlotte caught on pretty quick, amused at the mitten and fish idea. "I grew up for the most part in Maryville in the Upper Peninsula, right on the Canadian border. I'm a member of a Native American Tribe. I met my husband, Marc, when he came there assigned through Indian Health Service. He's a dentist. Marc is not practicing dentistry just now. I'm a student and a housewife, no children yet. We live with his family in Chevy Chase." Her natural ease in sharing herself with others warred with her instincts to guard, isolate and protect herself. To her own ear, her voice sounded flat when she described Marc. She knew in her gut she had nothing to fear from this woman, yet in an instinctual protective act, her eyes shifted around purposefully, afraid of doing something wrong. If just talking felt nice, then it ought to be okay, right? She wasn't sure anymore.

They relaxed a bit more, settling back into the chairs, enjoying the beautiful evening setting, away from the crush of the crowd inside.

"Tell me about your attire, Charlotte. I love the beautiful fabric you're wearing. Is it from your country?"

"Yes, it is," she said, looking down at her dress, adjusting some of the folds. "This is made by artisans in my country. Our cloth happens to be well known on the continent for intricate design and color. The bold designs don't always agree with my taste. I wear them anyway, probably out of loyalty to the weavers and dyers back home. In our small country in Central Africa, my husband is," she hesitated, then continued shyly, "with our government. We moved here for a rotation as he learns diplomatic skills and makes some contacts in Washington. We are most honored to be here. At least, that's what I'm told," she said sheepishly, "and I wish to do my best to see it through!"

She explained that her husband, Eddie, was busy with honorary appearances through the embassy, so she often tagged along. "He hopes to be trained in more substantial duties eventually."

As they conversed, Beth thoroughly enjoyed learning more about Charlotte and Eddie and their experiences as new residents in D.C. They joked about the terrible traffic, frequent roadblocks to allow important motorcades around the city, and never-ending invasion of tourists from all over the world.

"My dear, please forgive me for being so forward. I would love to know you better," Charlotte said. Beth understood her new friend ought to go back to mingling with the crowd soon. "I would love to hear more about your tribe. I used to read about American tribes, about tipis and canoes, and living off the land as do the villagers in my country. There must be more for you to tell me."

"I'd be honored to share what I know. There's definitely more to Native American tribal life than clothing and housing—though I don't claim to know everything."

"Maybe I can share a bit about natives in my country, too."

"I'd love to hear anything you could share about them. It's refreshing to meet you, Charlotte" Beth said. "Perhaps we could meet for lunch this week or are you too busy right now?"

"No, let's work it out—perhaps Wednesday, you could meet me in Georgetown? Give me your cell number and we'll finalize plans," Charlotte asked eagerly. They smiled at each other, truly taking each other in, basking in warm, fuzzy feelings, exchanging numbers.

Beth spotted Marc pointedly looking out the windows onto the terrace, obviously searching for her. He saw her, their eyes locked and he marched stiffly in her direction. His expression of annoyance announced his displeasure with her, keener than with words. Beth's stomach dropped, for she especially wanted not to risk his embarrassing her in front of her new friend.

"I'll call you tomorrow, Charlotte, and see you on Wednesday," she said over her shoulder, hastily trying to wind up their conversation. She then moved abruptly toward the advancing Marc, almost at a run, hoping to ward off any strident scene. She succeeded in circling the patio, drawing him away from Charlotte. Marc cut off her escape by grabbing her arm, dragging her aside and painfully twisting. She wanted to cry out in pain, but believed he would strike her if she gave him any provocation, despite being in public.

"Ouch, you're hurting me," she whispered, trying to escape his grasp. He gripped tighter.

"What occurred, making a spectacle of yourself?" he hissed. "I heard you practically knocked people over inside and then imposed yourself on strangers." He nodded toward the table she and Charlotte so recently occupied. She looked around to see if anyone looked suspicious of their exchange, spotting only Marc's mother watching them through huge glass doors, a scowl on her face and looking as if she smelled something foul, her eyes like slits, brow furrowed. Under other circumstances, Beth might consider her sullen frown humorous.

"What's the matter with you?" he growled at her. She knew it would be no use to try to explain. He let her go with a shove away from him. "I'll deal with you later," he spat caustically into her ear as he saw people starting to look their way. She rubbed her forearm, soothing away the redness and pain. Humiliation erupted all over her face.

"Get yourself to the car. We're leaving right now. Your behavior has embarrassed us again. We are too ashamed to remain here," he said through tightly clinched teeth. He glared at her so nastily, she dreaded the ride home.

Inside, her swirling stomach slowed a bit at the idea that at least she'd made a new interesting friend tonight. Charlotte would be her friend, not "their" friend, someone forced on her by Marc, who talked behind her back or reported every exaggerated flaw to Marc and his mother, but a true friend of her own choosing. She drew comfort in their brief encounter.

Chapter Three

The Gallery

She and Charlotte met the next week for lunch at a quaint soup and sandwich shop in Georgetown. D.C.'s young savvy crowd noisily vied for tables. They placed their orders at the counter, carrying their trays to a small table near the window.

"Beth, you shared that you attend school. I remembered later I failed to even ask, what is your major?"

"I'm still taking required courses at American University. I'm leaning toward education in art or art history. I completed a few courses back home in Michigan at Lake Superior State University. One day I'd love to go back home to teach kids. I hope to finish up my BFA here, then maybe go on for more."

Charlotte became excited. Her eyes widened, her arms waved in punctuation for her rapid reply, "I don't believe it! I'm in an art business, too. Actually,

I am working on it right now. My family has collected art for years. I'm working on bringing some pieces over here made by artists in my country. My sisters scour the countryside for unusual or beautiful artworks." She paused a moment before continuing her explanation. "We will be helping some of the superior artists by bringing their ethnic, rustic art here to sell and display. I hope selling them helps whole villages. At the same time, America can see their work and a glimpse of our culture as well." She swallowed her tea. "We plan to send the proceeds of sales back home to go directly to the artists, like an upscale artist's co-op gallery."

Beth nodded her interest obvious. "Wow, I envy you. You enjoy the best of all sides, showing interesting art here and helping your countrymen at the same time."

"I'm expecting a shipment from home in the next few weeks." She hesitated briefly, and then asked, "Could I impose on you to help me unpack and set up some displays? I couldn't pay you much right now, maybe more later. Others will stand by, assigned to help with heavy lifting. I need someone like you with an artistic flair. You possess style and an eye for color. You notice and comment on things around you. I appreciate that." Beth warmed inside, flattered and encouraged by Charlotte's praise. She'd not heard anything complimentary in so long, she blossomed. Usually she deflected or rejected praise for her own accomplishments.

"I'll be honored to help you, if you think I'd do you any good," she said softly. "I'm sure I could work time around my classes during the day. I must be available to my family at night, since they entertain or go out most evenings. I'd love to see your artists' works. Please, I don't require pay."

"You would be a huge help to me. I am determined to pay you, though. You must make a new bank account just for that money, to be used for emergencies or special things for yourself. Don't you dare tell your husband. A girl always should save her own mad money to fall back on if necessary." Charlotte giggled conspiratorially. Beth silently agreed, thinking of her own sad situation. It never occurred to her she'd need money. Somehow, she considered it disloyal to her husband to think in those terms.

The talk drifted to Charlotte's dreams for her gallery. In their relationship, Charlotte provided most of the talking while Beth listened, an arrangement meeting both their needs.

The next week when they went to look at the gallery, Beth saw a huge potential for display and sales of specialty crafts and artwork. On a side street in a fashionable DC neighborhood noted for boutique shops, the nearly empty gallery, with multi-room open spaces, big windows surrounded with a tiny yard garden, possibly could be polished into an art destination.

Beth learned Charlotte and her husband, Edward, the friendly, easy-going diplomat, lived above the gallery. Their home, beautifully restored, boasted an outside garden with a sturdy, decorative, wrought iron staircase leading to their rooms above. The first floor held huge windows to let in lots of natural light and invite potential customers along the street to see inside the cool and comfortable lobby. Outside a brass nameplate announced the entrance. Natural ivy-covered hedges, great for the city, with landscaping having the look and feel of postage stamp-size formal gardens had been laid out thoughtfully with terraced gravel paths, occasional seating, sculptures and several varieties of small trees.

"Your garden is lovely, Charlotte, I love the flowers you're growing, and the water feature. It's great to see the gardens from inside the gallery through those huge windows. It draws the eye in, like a peaceful hide-away," Beth observed as they walked the paths outside. Charlotte enjoyed showing Beth her gallery and gardens, beaming with pride.

"I like the recessed lighting and plush carpet, too," Beth gushed. She walked around several huge wooden crates that were just plunked down in the middle of the room.

"These must be the boxes you've been waiting for."

"Yes, and now that you're here, I'll call for assistance to come help us uncrate them and lift things out of the packing material. Here's a box cutter." Beth appreciated Charlotte's enthusiasm, if not her preparation. They needed much more than a box cutter to access the sturdy wooden shipping crates. "Sometimes packers go overboard. We'll need to search for the pieces among the paper and straw. Be on the lookout for fabric scraps wrapping the pottery, for sometimes it is as interesting as the pottery. I sometimes frame it or use it for decorating, too. I need your help with looking at everything and then suggesting how to display it."

Two people arrived, a strong young man with a crowbar who went right to work breaking open the crates, and a young woman who immediately started writing down the inventory. Charlotte announced Martine and Jasmine, less than an introduction, but yet a nod to good manners. Beth surmised they came over from the Embassy. They all spent the next three hours revealing goodies inside the boxes, working silently and constantly to uncrate precious cargo, setting the contents around the rooms. The scope and quality of the pottery enthralled her. Some art pieces stole her breath away, too.

Eventually, Charlotte called for a break. They all appreciated a breather. Charlotte and Beth sank into tired heaps onto the carpeted floor. The other two disappeared without a word.

"Where'd they go?" Beth asked.

"Oh, they'll be back in a while. They go back to the embassy compound for lunch. Lunch has been ordered to be delivered, if that's all right with you. It's from one of my favorite spots, so I hope you like it, too. We must choose some nice couches and chairs for this area, don't you think?" Charlotte said absently. "How do you like what you've seen so far?" she asked as they stretched out on the plush carpet.

"They're beautiful, the artistry and intricacy are remarkable. Each piece is unique. They appear specially selected to complement the others. Your sisters did a remarkable job of selecting them. I'm just imagining the dimensional pieces on some short shelves featured in the open room in the back left, with wall hangings and maybe various pedestal heights with green palmetto palm fronds hung between and around them."

As Beth spoke, Charlotte enjoyed watching her become animated about displaying the beautiful offerings from her beloved homeland.

"… and lighting projecting shadows with color gels between them. It would be clean and organic, thus keeping focus on the pieces." Beth hardly paused for breath. Charlotte loved Beth's ideas.

They ate lunch picnic style on the floor. Charlotte popped the cork on a good wine. They each topped the other with ideas, in artistic overload. They ate fruit and cheese chunks, chicken salad piled high on croissants, and white wine in plastic cups. After lunch, their two helpers magically returned. They all worked the remainder of the afternoon, emptying the boxes.

Beth remembered about four P.M., she must hurry or she'd be late getting home. "Oh my gosh, I must go right now. Traffic's going to be awful this time of day. I don't dare arrive late," Beth said, trepidation peppering her voice.

"He'll understand," Charlotte offered confidently.

Beth raised her eyebrows, saying quickly, "I doubt it." She ran to her parked car. She'd never arrive home and still be ready to leave again by six. She'd be in for another round with Marc.

She secreted away this pleasant afternoon in her nearly exhausted cache of good memories. She resolved to pay the price Marc would undoubtedly exact in exchange for these growing feelings of support and connection with Charlotte.

In the next several months, time with Charlotte became very precious to her. Otherwise, she endured way too much alone time.

She confided in Charlotte about her upbringing and her fractured life up to now. She said little about her relationship with Marc or what she endured most nights at home. Charlotte already guessed they experienced issues, yet remained kind enough not to quiz her on either the occasional sad moods or hastily covered bruises. She managed to keep them covered mostly, changing the subject if it came up. At those times, Charlotte obligingly allowed herself to become easily distractible.

Chapter Four

New York Gala

One long weekend, she and Marc traveled to New York City to attend a gala. They planned to stay several days, go to parties, and connect with suitable people. She wanted to see a show, but no shows occurred in Marc's hectic party schedule. The centerpiece of their trip, a charity affair, would be presided over by New York's elite. Marc and his mother warned her to look and behave her best. She dreaded it all, for history showed it would not be a good time for her.

Tonight, they dined at the chic, grand apartment of a very wealthy businessman named Vessage and his jet-set daughter, Gemma, for a small private dinner party. Twelve guests expected cocktails, a seated dinner, followed by aperitifs and cigars for the gentlemen.

"It's at dinners like this that new connections present themselves, Beth. This could affect our future so don't mess up," he told her, his ambitions ratcheted up by this invitation. He wanted to cultivate these people. Unclear what business or affairs he potentially had with these individuals, she wasn't privy to his plans.

She dressed in a fitted under-gown of deep golden yellow silk, overlaid with layers of dark-to-light yellow sheer, flowing fabric. She wore a huge, oval, golden yellow topaz choker pendant and earrings, a matching dinner ring and large oval topaz bracelet. She fanaticized that she looked like an exotic tropical bird. Upswept hair completed her look. Perfect nails and makeup gave her the resemblance of a pampered, society woman. Actually, she'd scraped clay from under those nails. She'd spent an inordinate amount of time on her hair and makeup. An astounding amount of moisturizer had been "glopped" onto her hands and body to make them magazine-beautiful.

Beth supposed these people knew each other, and remained evidently uninterested in meeting anyone new tonight. She resorted to her usual habit of scrutinizing furnishings and observing people. She walked over to hear a conversation across the room, where the hostess, Ms. Gemma Vessage, held court. That's about the only way to describe it, Beth reckoned. Four other men and women hung on her every utterance like lackeys, laughing a little too hard at her slightly snide descriptions of other people they all obviously knew. They fixated on Gemma, as if her approval meant everything. She surmised that unlike herself, Gemma wouldn't require hosing off or scraping clean of paint and clay. No, Gemma would employ a team of makeup and style experts caring for her every whim.

The group tittered at salacious gossip and outrageous innuendos in some secret shorthand known principally to them, which they rudely avoided sharing with a newcomer.

Gemma eventually became bored with the conversation, making the others strive harder for her attention, just short of panic to keep her engaged with them. She looked at Beth, speculatively scrutinizing her, and then motioned for her to join them. Gemma introduced Beth to the group. They exchanged superficial hellos and then lapsed into embarrassing silence, underscoring their lack of interest in her. They resumed their previous conversation about people unknown to Beth. She sipped her drink, continuing to smile, at a loss for a contribution of any fresh remarks or clever discourse.

Gemma, obviously accustomed to the pause in conversation, abruptly changed the subject, impaling Beth like a bug under a microscope of undesired examination. "So tell us, Beth, what do you do in Washington?"

Wanting to believe their interest, she launched into a generic recitation of her circumstances. "At present, I am a housewife and student. I work in a new gallery of African Native Art in Georgetown, and I attend American University. I'm actually doing my internship for teaching at a D.C. elementary school in the inner city."

"Really?" Gemma remarked, working up a little smirk, already dismissing Beth as anyone warranting further interest. "What do you think of our little collection here," she said, referring to some outstanding paintings adorning the walls of the apartment. Beth started to tell her but Gemma dismissed her with a wave of her hand, obviously already aware theirs was an impressive "little collection" of priceless, sought after art pieces.

"Aren't you scared to be in public school? How can you possibly do that? How does your husband allow that?" Gemma questioned her, almost in an accusing tone. Beth's heart sank, as she fired a look across the room toward Marc. He hardly needed a reason to stop her from finishing her internship. He could certainly make continuing very difficult for her, if he got wind of the notion that what she was doing may well not be cool in these people's eyes.

"I'm in no danger at the school," she defended. "The kids and their parents are great."

Gemma's interest in her passed. She turned her head to ask the woman next to her about her most recent tuck. Unabashedly, the woman launched into a shockingly explicit recounting of her surgery, which Beth found appalling. The group closed their conversational ranks, leaving her out.

She excused herself, making a hasty, embarrassed, exit from the group.

Beth prayed that Marc wouldn't learn about this conversation. Later at dinner, seated down the table from Gemma, she overheard the conversation among Gemma and her cronies.

Gemma looked at her directly with an evil smirk on her face and a malevolent look in her eye. She evidently enjoyed maligning others in order to feel better about herself. Beth was evidently the brunt of the joke shared at that end of the table, since they whispered to one another, then looked her direction.

Beth's cheeks flamed as she looked at Marc, hoping he remained oblivious. Realizing from the wicked expression on her face, Gemma knew Beth saw and heard the not-so-veiled references to do-gooders and misguided intentions, as if she dared Beth to confront her. At a loss to understand that some people took sadistic pleasure in the pain or embarrassment of others, Beth actually pitied them. *We now have your measure, Gemma Vessage. A truly gracious hostess or kind person wouldn't derive pleasure in another's discomfort. All this beauty and wealth around you, but you squander it with pettiness and ridicule of others. I don't wish you ill—you'll bring it on yourself with evil intentions, Gemma!*

Beth said nothing, shoving the elaborate food around her plate and covering her wine glass. She made it through this strained night.

She cringed, realizing the other social events scheduled for the weekend would also be shared with these cruel, thoughtless people. If it wouldn't backfire onto her, she'd speak her mind. So much for my big brush running with the rich and famous, she thought, preferring to go back home to Charlotte and people who remain good and kind.

After returning from New York, her mantra evolved into "seek harmony in life, move toward peace and balance in living."

Chapter Five
The Two Faces of Professor Engle

"This is beautiful work, Miss, uh," the attractive but distracted professor Engle dismissed her name with a wave of his hand, since he couldn't remember it. "You've captured something essential here, something ethereal." He cut off another student, who endured the misfortune to be snubbed mid-sentence with the professor. She had seen this classmate before, hanging around the art building, trying awfully hard to make an impression on Professor 'Dreamy.' Beth's head swiveled from the student back to the oblivious Professor Engle. The student's face momentarily twisted in recognition that he'd lost the professor's attention. She saw how upset the student became by being brushed off. His look of anger her startled her. Professor Engle seemed unconcerned about angering or insulting anyone. She tried to signal her apology to the guy, but he gave a disgusted shake of his head. His face then turned entirely neutral and he strode away.

Professor Engle demanded her attention. "Thank you so much, Professor Engle. Should these brown tones should be deeper or longer?"

"I wouldn't change it, just go ahead to finish it. Let's fire it by itself." She couldn't help but feel a bit smug, since that was the ultimate honor for a student.

"Okay," she said sheepishly, knowing her fellow students would not be happy to have to wait while her work was in the kiln alone.

Professor Dreamy, as all the girls called him, gave her one of his electric looks. He doled out his famous smiles, the ones he used for impressing the gullible female students who became captivated by his mystique. Before this moment, she'd just been another student in the department, undistinguishable from many others.

He met her eyes now, and his features softened, turning his mega-watt smile right on her. She cringed, half expecting him to make some inappropriately personal or suggestive comment.

"I understand you're involved with a gallery downtown. Why do you suppose I never heard about you before now?"

Beth shrugged, both relieved and offended. "I don't know, I've been here, every class. You should come by the gallery some time. We have some very beautiful examples of ..." Her voice trailed off as he noticeably lost interest.

He interrupted her. "I'm sure. Let's meet for coffee one day this week. I'd like to discuss it." Her natural politeness kicked in. She agreed to meet him on Friday at the gallery.

His previously stellar smile devolved as he moved on.

She didn't like the direction his interest seemed headed. Why now? What did he want? Did he think she would give him free gallery space? Did he want something else from her?

It became clearer why they hadn't met before now. She didn't like his demeanor in class so much anyway. He criticized students or ignored them altogether, just as he'd done with her up to now. It saddened her that while he possibly could have something to teach her, she'd keep him at arm's length. He would do better with those students who coveted his attention, like that poor sap earlier. If he pushed her on wanting space in their gallery, she could resort to blaming Charlotte for wanting only native artists on display.

On Friday, he showed up late. She saw he brought a portfolio with him, eagerly looking around, but not seeing the work already there.

She gave him the tour, however he showed little interest in the native art on display. He kept up a one-sided dialogue on the treasure his particular sensibilities brought as a gift to the artistic world.

She struggled to maintain her manners. She tried to nod at his one-sided dialogue, feigning interest. He amused himself so grandly, he hardly noticed her attention lagged. She somehow managed to turn him down gracefully for a solo exhibit.

She spoke to Charlotte about it later. "He is so full of himself, how does he survive? His ego is all-encompassing. I don't believe he even understood what is at the gallery. What's worse, I'm going to endure being nice to him as long as I'm in school. He's a professor, after all, in the Department I want to obtain my Masters."

"You're not required to like him," commiserated Charlotte, "but you must determine to remain positive with him. You said he can teach you things, so play that angle, why don't you? Just don't close off your potential. You need him right now."

"You're so right. With my own art, it's a matter of knowing in my heart what's good. It's the difference between training and just knowing. Maybe it's a native thing, where feeling and spirit coexist. It's so different from Western culture, which is just the opposite, less feelings, all think and do."

"I understand the subtlety. I think that's one of the little surprises you bring to all things, Beth, how you live your spirituality. That's one of the first things I sensed about you, and what makes me feel a kinship with you. Don't fret over this shallow man. He'll be gone from your life in the wink of an eye." Charlotte's advice comforted and challenged her.

She tried to tell Marc about her classes. He rebuffed listening to her until she tried to tell him about Professor Dreamy and the disappointing meeting in the gallery. Marc became focused on the "other man," as he called the professor and any other male to whom she spoke, blowing even minor exchanges completely out of proportion. He became obsessed imagining any man she might be around, until she became exhausted trying to rationally explain things. He accepted no explanation for his irrational conclusions. Eventually, she stopped talking about her classes altogether, as any small information became an excuse for him to berate her.

"They won't notice how bossy and frigid you are right away. Must you embarrass me by playing the whore with those teenagers, too? How can you look at yourself in the mirror, knowing your whoring behaviors are seen by everyone around you?"

When he started taking her books, class notes, or projects, hiding them from her, she refrained from arguing, just spent more time looking for them. However, when he started destroying them, she learned not to bring any work into the house. Often after a combatant morning, he greeted her facetiously warmly, his demeanor ingratiating, barely tolerable, until the dam broke and violence erupted. He no longer even apologized for it afterward. She grew to prefer the morning litany of her faults since the evening counterpart usually proved much more physically punishing. Anything she said carried potential for escalating his angry outbursts. She organized her best to work around him. Everyone near them turned a deaf ear or blind eye, although her bruises the next day ought to signal something. Nobody noticed or at least, no one commented.

She held her ground about continuing to go to school. She progressed a little farther along toward her goal to finish college and continue studying for an advanced degree in art history and art education. She found her niche in helping others discover their own creativity, encountering other professors besides Professor Dreamy, including her favorite, Professor Bizant, who encouraged her development as an artist. It made life tolerable for a little while, but she saw no end, no respite in store.

Chapter Six

Transition

Several months back, surviving Marc's most violent attack, she limped into the women's shelter after release from the hospital. At last facing the truth, she had to go there to survive. She couldn't go home again.

Charlotte helped her make the move to the shelter and insisted that leaving Marc was a matter of life and death now. Numb, emotionally spent, she allowed Charlotte to make the arrangements for her. Although feeling vulnerable, wanting out from under the violence, yet not wanting to break her wedding vows, she finally accepted she couldn't maintain it both ways. The shelter was more than just a roof. She was guided through the painful process of separating, looking at options, recapturing her self-esteem and rebuilding her life.

Now that the biggest hurdle, the escape from danger to safety was accomplished, room developed in her life for other things, like being balanced emotionally, letting herself feel things again—perhaps eventually some happiness, too. Had she ever been happy or sad, or angry, even? They'd all been refined out of her or else, she let them go to survive. She also knew her connection to nature got lost along the way. She counted it as a victory when she spontaneously cried from normal sadness or happiness again.

She accepted the fact that the divorce would likely be ugly. She expected to spend a while detached from emotions, to let go eventually of conflict with Marc and his family.

She wanted to rebuild confidence in herself, to remake her life. She wanted peace.

One quiet day at the shelter, she and Caroline, her counselor, talked about the divorce over coffee at the kitchen table. She confided in Caroline.

"Yes, money is nice." Beth admitted. "Cash is good, no doubt." She folded her hands on the table. "But I lost much more than things, Caroline. I also lost pride, trust and belief in people. I can't see myself emotionally involved with anyone ever again. I have so much rage, so much sadness, not just for his hurting me physically. That's healed now." Caroline sighed, reached across the table to cover Beth's clenched fists with her warm, open hands, as she continued, "It's his purposefully twisting my mind and then manipulating me—that I can't forget."

"Never say never, Beth. Look how many of your

friends reached out to you in your time of need. Your old friends, like Charlotte, and your new friends—the women and the caring men you've met here, remember how they opened up to embrace you. We all see how well you're recovering." Beth appreciated hearing those words. Tears welled up, threatening to flood down her face, but didn't.

"Once you forgive yourself for being human, for taking risks and making mistakes, your healing comes naturally. Remember, anyone can be fooled—even you. Forgiveness is your new mantra, girlfriend." The word "forgiveness" hung there like a nagging insect, one she wanted to brush away.

"You won't always need to fight non-productive thoughts from creeping into your mind. Just acknowledge them—release anger as you go or it bogs you down. The word for today is GOOD! Move ahead with good intentions, good thoughts, and positive actions in your life. Claim the good before you, your path is filled with good!"

"How will I ever keep this going after I leave you positive people?"

"You'll accomplish it for yourself," Caroline said, "I'll be proud of you, every step of the way. You'll be helping others, too." Beth perked up hearing such praise, sitting a little straighter, head a little higher. "You're going to remember how you've been helped. You'll pass it on, I'm sure. Anyway, you're here now, staying until the end of the month," Caroline looked around the kitchen.

"You and the rest of the staff plan to come to my graduation from college next week, yes?" Beth asked, wanting their conversation to continue.

"We're all looking forward to seeing you cross the stage in your cap and gown. You're generous to invite everyone. Many of our women never see anyone graduate from anything, so it's a real treat for us," Caroline said, refilling their coffee cups from the always-ready coffee pot in the clean, tidy kitchen. "Has Ms. Albion told you yet she is throwing a celebration for you at her office?" she asked. "I hear Charlotte is sending some catering staff from their embassy in your honor. So it's going to be a pretty fancy shindig."

"It means a lot to me for all of you to be here," Beth admitted.

"Just so you'll be properly surprised, the kids from the shelter practiced a special song to thank you for all the free art classes you gave them. They love you. You've touched so many people with your gifts of art and creativity, Beth. You already know how many are helped therapeutically to express themselves creatively during your classes. You've been their angel in so many ways. The kids just want to give back. Accept it, hear it, incorporate it. Don't push appreciation aside. It's also part of your healing. Receive the appreciation sincerely offered."

Beth listened to her friend, practicing smiling all the way down inside this time.

Beverly Waters McBride

Chapter Seven

Maryland: Reclamation Yours, Mine and Ours

Beth sat in her car waiting for Charlotte, feeling numb. She wanted just to go in and out of Marc's house, not her house or their house, but Marc's house. She wrote down a list of things she needed. Time would be too short to look for anything, heck, she doubted she'd even be allowed in. Charlotte would be with her for moral support. Perhaps they could divide and conquer, each taking a piece of the list. Anything she came away with would be a victory.

Charlotte's car pulled up behind hers, a man in the vehicle with her. She hoped Charlotte's husband, Eddie, was staying clear of this. It couldn't be good for his diplomatic reputation if it got ugly.

Charlotte stepped out of her car and then re-introduced the man with her as Martine, from her country. Beth remembered Martine from unpacking at the gallery, which helped her relax a little. He looked as if he might be able to handle himself in almost any situation. He reminded her of her old beau, Dan. Dan could fade or stand out as needed, too.

"Don't worry about Martine, he'll just hang back, or be a distraction, or whatever we need," Charlotte said. Her confidence helped Beth gird up for the coming ordeal, too.

"You sure we ought to try this? I'm afraid they ...," Beth's voice trailed off, imagining all the potential hurt that might be unleashed.

"What are they going to do to you that they haven't already inflicted, Beth, what? Might they talk mean to you, or belittle you? They did that already. Are they going to hurt you? Martine and I aren't going to allow that. You've already experienced the worst from them. This little operation is liberating some things you need to move on with your life. You aren't going to let these people hold power over you anymore. Right? Besides, you're just claiming possession of your own things." She spared a moment to thank Charlotte silently for her strength today.

Charlotte spoke confidently, "Now let's go, girl, and reclaim your stuff!"

As Beth shakily inserted the key in the lock, Charlotte whispered to her, "Martine has our back, so let's go directly up to your room, OK? Oh, I brought some plastic bags if we need them." She held out a handful of black plastic bags, not the set of matching Luis Vuitton she used the last time she traveled.

The tumble of the key in the lock echoed in her ears. She winced, feeling like a turtle sticking out its head, wary, ready for withdrawal back into her shell at the least provocation. They immediately marched up the stairs. They made it almost to the top of the stairs when Marc's mother called out. "Beth, what are you doing here? Where have you been? We've been looking for you everywhere." Beth doubted that. Mother Morrison sputtered, outrage toward Beth bleeding over into her shrill, squawking voice.

Beth stopped, momentarily frozen, but Charlotte kept moving, grabbed Beth's arm, easing her forward. Beth slowed slightly to deal with Mrs. Morrison, but Charlotte maneuvered them around the shrieking, wildly gesturing woman.

"Look, we're here just to pick up a few essentials," Charlotte announced .

"I need to pick up some clothes and personal items. If you'll step aside, I'll find my things and be gone," she added from her daze.

Mrs. Morrison fumed in the doorway while Beth quickly circled the room gathering up the few mementoes she remembered bringing with her. Meanwhile, Charlotte unabashedly scoured the closet, throwing clothes, shoes, and purses into the plastic bags. Beth went to her dresser, lingering only briefly over the expensive perfumes bottles in favor of mementos she'd squirreled away in the drawers, out of Marc's sight or comment.

Martine materialized. "May I borrow your car key? I'll carry these bags down. Be right back," he said.

"Sure, thank you," she said, too spacey to really register what he said. He picked up four huge plastic bags, two in each hand, then raced down the stairs, returning quickly.

Marc's mother finally collected herself. She stood in front of Beth, saying, "You'll not seize this," as she grabbed some wedding gift figurines out of Beth's hands. Beth let them go, and instead reached behind her, picking up her jewelry box, passing it behind Mother Morrison to Charlotte, who bagged it. Then she deflected around Mrs. Morrison again to collect defiantly those perfume bottles she'd passed on earlier. As soon as Mrs. Morrison laid the figurines down, Charlotte swooped in, grabbed them up again, situating them inside a bag by the door, where Martine grabbed up another load. A flustered Mother Morrison practically turned around in circles, comically sputtering "Oh my, my, my-oh-my." Beth almost felt sorry for her again. Mrs. Morrison, recovered, called out for the servants. None came running immediately.

Beth took a look around her former prison and saw they'd pretty well picked the carcass clean. Anything she valued or wanted no longer existed here. They needn't stick around any longer to confront the staff.

Descending the stairs one last time, Martine behind them with yet more bags, Charlotte carried Beth's evening gowns over one arm and a warm winter coat over the other. Beth carried personal items inside a huge woven bag and a stack of household items wedding gifts.

When they paused outside the door, Mrs. Morrison closed it behind them in a window-shaking slam, almost catching Martine's back.

Beth and Charlotte looked at each other, then burst out laughing, a spontaneous release of tension, which easily turned emotional. Charlotte playfully nudged her on the shoulder, which made them both start dropping the items they held. Beth slid to her knees, right on the sidewalk, laughing, surrounded by a circle of dropped household items. Martine whispered in Charlotte's ear, then he disappeared, like a ghost.

"Some other good news has developed for you, Beth. What you don't know is that Martine is an expert in "covert operations." He prepared a bit of pre-strike homework on your behalf. He secured a few things for you from a secret safe. Here's the items he identified as your documents."

With that, Charlotte handed Beth a sheaf of papers including her birth certificate, Social Security card, passport, bonds and sales receipts. She never dreamed she'd get these back. Especially if Marc, his mother or their lawyers figured a way to keep them from her.

"Oh, there's these, too." Charlotte reached out, holding a double handful of her good jewelry, all in a jumble. Beth saw some of her favorite pieces entwined, including her beautiful blue topaz necklace, her favorite tanzanite and diamond broach, her ruby combs, and other precious jewelry pieces she never dreamed she'd see again. She knew these were locked up in the safe.

"How? When?" She looked inquisitively at Charlotte, as she looked around for Martine.

"Martine has some unusual abilities. You don't need to worry—we ensured proof that each piece is yours. Anyway, possession is nine-tenths of the law is what I've heard."

Beth laid out each piece on top of her wedding gift towels to look at them.

Charlotte helped Beth stand up, gather up the goods, and load both cars. She would store her things at Charlotte's. Beth feared hell to pay because of the jewelry and the papers having been "liberated" out of the safe. Her divorce would be difficult enough without antagonizing Marc.

She hated the whole contested divorce thing, wanting to avoid confronting him or his family, or his lawyers. She only wanted out at this point.

She remained conflicted. She'd made vows, for cripes sake. What about those? Then the small voice of reason piped up, saying, "You didn't sign on to be abused." Yeah. She'd lived through the conflict, although she was a bit worse for the wear.

She calmed a bit after conferring with Ms. Albion, her divorce lawyer. The shelter recommended her, a women's advocate with the reputation as a divorce pit bull. They joked at the shelter that Ms. Albion ate opposing council for breakfast. Ms. Albion, short of stature, wore tailored suits in neutral colors. Her facial features could be described as plain, while her sharp, sparkling eyes told of her intelligence. Her manner conveyed unlimited energy. She had a stunning grasp of the law and undoubtedly loved her work. Mrs. Albion feared no one, agreed to work for Beth, and set about to prepare for whatever Marc's lawyers dished out.

Still hurting emotionally and drained from her experiences, Beth appreciated Ms. Albion's already accomplished preparation for the many meetings required with Marc and his team of lawyers. "I usually manage to obtain what you deserve," Ms. Albion told her. "All you need to do is be there, respond only if I ask you to answer a question. You let me do the talking."

Beverly Waters McBride

Chapter Eight
Maryland: Confrontation

"Won't you please take a seat? I'll let Mr. Mort know you're here," the pretty receptionist with the big innocent face and tight pink sweater told them from behind her glassed-in cage. They followed her gesture of invitation, turning toward the otherwise vacant waiting room. They all three sat on the edges of the offered chairs, anxious over the encounter to come. Beth kept her head down, although her eyes darted around the room, too nervous to grasp it all at once.

Designed to intimidate, the space reeked of power and old money, tempered by a nod to southern hospitality and good manners. Usual office aromas—a blend of furniture polish, ink, paper, brewing coffee and some kind of floral air freshener—hung faintly in the air. The waiting room held the requisite thick, plush carpeting, oversized, heavy dark wood furniture and deep comfy chairs. The room gave the appearance of little use, as if no one actually waited there often. Occasional tables, covered with neat rows of current, yet untouched magazines, like Time, People, and Sports Illustrated, punctuated several seating groupings, while healthy green potted ferns reached out in all directions. Muted lighting glowed from low table lamps with big cream-colored shades.

Unseen staff answered the intermittent buzz of a phone, as periodically a file drawer slammed closed. They heard a muted churn of machinery from a copier working out of sight in a back room.

"Must we wait long?" Beth asked, making small talk in her nervousness, absently gnawing the inside of her lip, alternatively clamping her jaws so tight, her teeth actually hurt.

Caroline, her counselor-turned-friend from the shelter shrugged. She came to give Beth moral support, while Ms. Albion worked on her behalf and would do all the talking.

As hoped, they weren't kept long. Beth, her shaking knees scarcely holding her up, felt lightheaded as she rose. All the same, she pasted on a small, polite smile.

"Ladies, please follow me into the conference room," the motherly, gray-haired assistant with half glasses on a chain around her thin neck said, leading the way, as they dutifully followed her through the maze of law offices. "Mr. Mort, Mr. Morrison and the other gentlemen already wait for you," she explained as she gestured them into the large conference room, centered with a heavy granite-topped conference table and high back chairs on rollers, stamped with gleaming brass studs. Trays on each side held clear pitchers of water. "They're here, Mr. Mort," the woman graciously addressed the older gentleman at the head of the table, before she stepped aside to let the women in. Beth looked longingly at the only way out, but the cardigan-and-pearls woman shut the door behind them. There would be no escape now.

Mr. Mort rose, gesturing them to be seated in the empty chairs across the table. Marc, her soon to be ex-husband, God willing, along with his jackal-like team of resourceful divorce attorneys, were all dressed in black power suits, pastel ties, with crisp white shirts and shined shoes. Evidently, they joked among themselves about last night's game. They stopped their relaxed, water cooler quarterbacking when the three women arrived. The entire row of six men stood as the women found their seats. Beth noticed that Marc, her soon to be ex, required prompting by one of his attorneys to stand, not looking so happy about it. If the collective lawyers, showing typical boy's club arrogance as they sat around the table, held any indication of knowing Ms. Albion's rep as a fighter for victims, they didn't reveal it. According to Ms. Albion, lawyers usually know their potential court opponents, and the tactics expected.

Ms. Albion told Beth ahead of time she'd already fielded a few contentious phone conferences with Marc's lawyers. This was to be a conference, more a settlement mediation, and not a hearing or official proceeding. She told Beth she saved surprises for the other side, but hadn't been specific about the information she planned to introduce. Ms. Albion maintained her brave and forthright, let-the-negotiations-begin, attitude.

As they settled across the cold granite table, women on one side, men on the other, the irony of boys and girls on opposite sides of the table was not lost on her.

Beth's whole body shook. The air conditioning blew directly onto the room's occupants, leaving her uncomfortably cold. She wished now she'd brought a sweater. Caroline, her competent counselor/friend, held her icy hand under the table in warm support that helped calm her a bit.

Beth only wanted out of the marriage intact. Going back to Marc's house to retrieve her personal things and important papers was either reckless or brave, depending on your point of view. Just worrying about it, frustration rose to anger, so she wedged her shaking hands under her thighs, hoping to regain control of her traitorous, seesawing, emotions. Beth always seemed to live with doom just looming around the next corner and today was no different.

Her stress hindered her hearing, as they bogged down again in petty detail. She came back to attention at words uttered by Marc's attorney, Mr. Mort, "… Native American …"

Beth sensed a nudge under the table, and Ms. Albion's voice became strident.

"Gentlemen, I am sure you are not implying Mrs. Morrison's Native American heritage in any way factors in to the deplorable events of her marriage to Mr. Morrison. I'm positive you do not intend to introduce any further reference to her culture or heritage into these negotiations. Inserting a far over-reaching, extraneous argument where it does not belong, " she pursed her lips, speculatively, "would be discriminatory, perhaps subject to action in another arena."

Ms. Albion leaned over whispering for her ears only, "Look outraged." Beth reacted, frowning and straightening her blouse. Beth gave them her best try at a facial expression of disgust—at least she hoped it conveyed distain. Across the table, the frat boys, as she considered them, exhibited the good manners now to appear sheepish.

Ms. Albion stared into the eyes of each man across from her, one at the time, as if daring them to speak. Each of them in turn revealed their nervousness by darting eyes away, one loosening a collar, another wiping a brow, a third, covering his mouth with his fingers, another pouring a glass of water.

Mrs. Albion mocked, "Yes, you knew better than to hope that argument would fly and some of you, at least, regret it already. Did you imagine I would let that slide?"

Even Mr. Mort, Marc's lead attorney, shuffled the papers in front of him, quickly saying, "Moving on ..."

His lawyers threw outlandish arguments in her direction, like accusations of infidelity, and worse. Ms. Albion repudiated the allegations, point by point.

"We understand Mrs. Morrison and her henchmen broke into the Morrison home, assaulted her frail mother-in-law and stole valuable items," one of them claimed.

Unruffled, Mrs. Albion set the record straight. "First, you well know that is false, as Mrs. Morrison could not break in to her own home. Her companions, hardly henchmen, indeed both well-respected dignitaries, assisted her in carrying out her personal items, clothing and cosmetics."

"The elder Mrs. Morrison was not touched or harmed in anyway. Mrs. Morrison, here, a resident in the house, having a key, was entitled to legal and proper access to her personal belongings." Mrs. Albion stopped for a breath.

"We understand jewelry was removed as well," Mr. Mort snarled.

"Do you hold any statement or proof that Mrs. Morrison obtained any item not her own by gift or prior to the marriage?" Mrs. Albion asked Mr. Mort. Beth saw that Marc squirmed. Mr. Mort noticed, too, and backed off, trying another tack.

"There is a matter of alleged infidelity, and hiding assets," he pressed, matter-of-factly.

"For the record," she stated as she looked at the stenographer pointedly, "Mrs. Morrison, quite the opposite, has no history of infidelity. If you retain some proof beyond your far-fetched claim, please bring it forth." Mrs. Albion countered by insisting they produce evidence of their claims. They, of course, asserted none.

Innuendo from Marc's team of lawyers grated on her nerves. Her stomach churned, agitating like a washing machine, grinding, twisting and turning.

Then they began talking money. Silently shocked to hear such large sums of money bandied about, Beth cared nothing about their money. She would settle to walk away from the marriage, to be out from under the abuse. The shelter counselors and her lawyer remained adamant that she needed to stand fast, to ask for what she required to establish a new life. But to her, no amount of Marc's money could make up for her loss of self-esteem and confidence during their three-year marriage.

As the meeting wore on Marc's face, which started out neutral, cocky even, became twisted and dark. Still sensitive to his every mood change, she knew him to be seething inside. His malevolent gaze never wavered from Beth's face, his fixed stare holding all the venom of which she knew him capable. She swallowed, wiping her damp hands on her skirt. She thanked heaven she didn't have to face him alone tonight.

Ms. Albion dramatically pulled out a sheaf of paperwork. It contained pictures taken of Beth's face and body when she first arrived, bruised and battered, at the women's abuse shelter. Ms. Albion exaggeratedly laid the pictures one by one across the table, Polaroid's and five-by-sevens, showing Beth's battered condition. One of Marc's lawyers recoiled, coughed, then turned away quickly.

"Notice this wound on Mrs. Morrison's face from the belt-whipping she sustained on November twentieth," Ms. Albion stated, letting the photo float to the tabletop. "I know this is uncomfortable for you, Mrs. Morrison. Would you please show us the scar on your face." The room quieted, no one else moved.

Numb at this point, Beth lifted her hair, then turned her head for all to see. She felt ashamed of the puffy red line along her cheek. Her head pounded and her whole face reddened. Censure from old, nagging voices inside her head reared, whispering, "Nice women don't bear scars like that." Caroline compassionately eased her arm along the back of Beth's chair, causing her to almost melt in appreciation for her friend's support at that moment.

Ms. Albion continued, "Here is the succession of injuries: dislocated arm in December, broken ribs on February fourteenth—may I point out not a Valentine but a broken rib on that occasion; back injuries and severe bruising from February twenty-third. Here is the report of internal bleeding from March eighth of this year, which resulted in her second hospitalization. After this assault, she was forced to seek much needed shelter from her husband's increasingly violent attacks." She stood back, pursed her lips and clasped her hands in front of her. "This sad history amounts to persistent and purposeful, long-term physical attacks perpetrated by Mr. Morrison. Before us is an irrefutable indictment, visible proof of persistent and escalating violence imposed upon her by her husband. This, gentlemen, is not some accident-prone housewife, or her husband's misguided correction attempt. No one—please, hear me well—no one deserves this kind of treatment and certainly not at the hand of someone pledged to love and protect her.

Mrs. Albion gestured at the array of proof, letting the pictures achieve the talking. Like a skilled huntress circling for the kill, she directed their attention to the damning photos again. "Please look again at the pictures, gentlemen, at the tearing, bruising and scarring visible forevermore on her battered body. Here is documentation from the hospitals, paramedics, and doctors treating my client for significant, devastating injuries, including sworn affidavits over the last two years. This repeated violence, gentlemen, is why we are here." She made eye contact with Mr. Mort as her hand swept again across the array of photos and papers now on the table. He tugged on his necktie, cocked his head aside, and raised his eyebrows toward Marc. Another of Marc's lawyers pushed back his chair from the table as if to distance himself from the evidence spread out on the table.

"Even after all of this, Mrs. Morrison is not vengeful, nor retaliatory. She deserves her day in court. We, in fact, look forward to it. However, my client may be willing to discuss other options. We anticipate turning over this documentation to the proper authorities. We anticipate filing a subsequent civil suit in the very near future. However, if spared further trauma in favor of a fair, equitable, non-contested divorce settlement, she may be willing to consider that as well." All eyes turned to Marc, who lowered his eyes and angrily jammed his hands into his pockets, letting his pinched, tight mouth reveal his frustration. Was he angry with himself over the violence or just angry that his deeds had been brought into the open?

"If you intend to move forward, stalling the settlement, we can certainly go that route, also.

I'll be happy to respond further on our end. The restraining order is here. Sir, you are served." Mrs. Albion pushed the papers halfway across the table. No one reached for them, although they all looked at them. No one wanted to pick up that hot potato, evidently.

"With that, gentlemen, we bid you good day. Please call me with your counter," Ms. Albion stood. She and Caroline followed her lead. She motioned for the ladies to precede her out the door.

Beth looked back to the row of lawyers still hovering around the table. Marc, slumping as if the wind had been knocked out of his arrogant body, whirled around in his fancy chair, his back toward them. The back of his neck practically glowed red, betraying his red-faced chagrin. No one wanted to talk sports with him now.

Even then, despite the hurt, the injury, the betrayal, she unaccountably wanted to reach out to him, to comfort him. She characteristically wanted no one to suffer, not even him. Thank goodness, Caroline stepped behind her, blocking her view as they exited the office.

Walking out that door, she emerged on the other side without the clinging, gooey yoke of her empty marriage, misplaced loyalty to Marc, or crumbled expectations for the future, which had kept her imprisoned. What did she glean from this meeting? She knew she had to go through it to move on, yes. She vowed to feel differently—no more dreaming, no more wanting someone to assume care of her. From this point on, she'd resume care of herself.

Chapter Nine

Georgetown Shocker

"Absolutely not! This won't do at all. It's too far away from the transit stop and it's too far from any store or even a restaurant. Beth, this is not for you," Charlotte said emphatically, obviously irritated and a bit testy today. They walked away from a pricey but small apartment she may perhaps have rented, if Charlotte proved less cranky. Beth sensed Charlotte wasn't truly committed to the hunt.

Charlotte and Beth circumnavigated the city, looking for an apartment so she could move out of the shelter at the end of the month. Beth expected to continue volunteering with the children of the women still living there, while looking for a "real" job, waiting for her teaching certifications. She would be getting her Master's degree in art history and education next week, then finishing her art therapy internship soon after. Since she could now afford her own place, thanks to the work of Ms. Albion and her successful arguments, she wanted to allow other women without the newly-acquired-in-her-divorce means to have coveted transition space through the shelter. She could use her own resources for her future, now that she possessed some.

"Well, we must find something!" Beth said plaintively. "I want something artsy, with enough space to work and live, you know?" Charlotte continued to frown. She'd be happy with a lot less than Charlotte evidently wanted for her.

Charlotte wouldn't let her consider the apartment they'd just looked at. "I understand perfectly, Beth. You don't need to settle for bad lighting in bad neighborhoods. Let's stop for something to drink. I want to spring an idea on you." They ducked into a little basement rathskeller near the gallery for refreshments. Charlotte confirmed that something else consumed her mind, which would account for her frequent daydreaming lately. After they ordered, Charlotte sipped the herbal tea in front of her. She looked at Beth with a furrowed brow.

"Things are going to change soon for you and me," she said gloomily. "I have news. It's all good, except that what affects me affects you, too. The fact is we're going to go back to Africa soon." Her serious manner betrayed how hard this was for her to discuss. Beth's face registered her denial. Charlotte continued, "In the meantime, we must move back into the Embassy complex." Shocked, Beth tried to understand, realizing what a huge change this signaled, for all of them. Her first reaction became a shattering "No-o-o." She listened to her friend, taking in her news.

"All this presents me with a dilemma. I need someone to undertake running the gallery. It just has to be you, Beth. We won't be using the apartment. You would simply be doing us a huge favor to live in it. It's not good for it to be empty." Charlotte added, "You could set up a studio there for drawing and your pottery wheel. There's room to store your work there, too. Beth, my dear, I trust you with the gallery, especially after we leave the country. I count it as a huge favor to be able to turn this over to you. I hesitate to ask, because I know what a commitment it is. The only way I'd allow it is if you'll become my partner and my proxy here. I want you to receive long-term financial rewards, as well as an artistic stake in the business. Let me sign over the property to you. If you want, we'll write it up so you purchase the building and the gallery from us. In time, it would all be yours. Please ponder that awhile, as I tell you the rest."

"The earnest look on your face could wring sympathy from a stone, Charl. How could I possibly refuse you, after all you've done for me?" she said, reassuring her friend that they could work something out.

"I've not been exactly forthcoming with you up to now," Charlotte confessed, a sheepish expression on her face. "For me, time away from obligations at home, to spend some carefree, happy, creative time with Eddie, has been an especially nice, once-in-a-lifetime hiatus for me. I've always known the time Eddie and I spent here would be an idyllic honeymoon for the two of us." She paused. "You see, when we return to Africa, Eddie will be crowned as King in our country. He assumes the throne from his father."

Dumbfounded, Beth asked, "Then, you … ?"

"Yes." Now shy, Charlotte admitted, "I'm gonna be the Queen." She laughed at that, eyes sparkling, her hand covering her mouth. "I enjoy the status of princess in my country now," she explained, almost giddy to be sharing her secret. "Once Eddie is in power, I will be his queen, at his side for life. Imagine me, a queen?" They both bent toward one another, smiling, to clutch hands across the table, chuckling as close friends, relishing the amazing good fortune awaiting Charlotte. She looked relieved to be sharing the information at last.

Beth imagined all the good Charlotte would achieve for her beloved people.

"We'll only have a short time here, maybe two months at most until we leave. That is why I hate to press you for a decision on this now. I must move back to the compound at the embassy right away. Perhaps you haven't noticed the security guards, who suffer the unfortunate task of providing my security. I warned them to stay out of sight and don't bother me. You'll probably recognize Martine, if he shows himself."

Beth automatically pivoted her head around, but saw only various people to scrambling from her view.

"I know this is a lot to grasp. I have one more bit of news to share with you, my friend, which is probably what launched everything in motion." She reached across the table again, right there in the basement restaurant, to clutch Beth's hands.

"I'm pregnant." They looked at each other, stone-faced, until Beth broke into laughter. She was overjoyed that her very good friend had transitioned into motherhood. Beth and Charlotte both squealed, jumped up and hugged.

"She's expecting!" Beth announced to the other restaurant patrons nearby. Even strangers broke into applause, offering faint shouts of congratulations before turning back to their sandwiches and beer.

"This is wonderful news, Charlotte. What else can I say? You must be thrilled! What does Eddie say? Does your family know? How far along are you? I'm so happy for you, for you both! This is just terrific," she gushed, wanting to know everything all at once.

Beth saw the various security people who had surged forward during all the noise slowly back away again into the shadows. They settled back down again in their seats, concentrating again on their meal. Beth distractedly wondered about the changes their friendship might encounter from here on out.

"Eddie is thrilled. To father an heir so early in our marriage is a good omen for him. He will be such a good father, he loves his home and family. Of course, he'll be very busy with state matters, so we all ensure our part to support him. This little one will be loved, not just by his family, but the whole country. I'm scared, yet happy. They want me to travel back soon, so Eddie is tying up loose ends in his work here. I don't want to close, since what we do here is too important back there. That is why just to entrust it all into your hands would ease my mind so." Charlotte sought out Beth's eyes. "I will accept what you decide about the gallery, but please plan on taking the apartment above, OK? I'd give you the building outright. However, I know you're such a stickler, you wouldn't accept it like that. I could leave your name on it without your permission, you know, and there's not much you could do about it, after all. So, let me help you, especially since you're helping us." She paused for breath. "So, what is your thinking?"

"I'd be honored to assume care of the gallery. I'll carry out everything in my power to see that it continues and succeeds. The offer of the apartment above is too fabulous to pass up. Isn't your little sister, Emmie, going to come over here to go to school soon? They certainly know about the art in the gallery, since they sent it over, don't they? Why don't we leave options open for me to eventually hand it off to one or both of your very capable little sisters in the future."

Charlotte said, "You know the business and you show how much you love it every day. You've earned the opportunity to take over. We all want to see it in your hands. I know it's asking a lot of you, but in my heart I know it's the right thing."

Beth objected no further. "For now, don't you worry about a thing." Beth grasped Charlotte's hands across the lunch table and bent low, looking intently into her friend's eyes. "Just concentrate on growing a happy, healthy baby. You've given support and faith, through thick and thin. We will always be friends, Charlotte."

"It's settled then. You will be expected to attend the coronation. Plan to come for three weeks before. I'll need you with me, to keep me sane. I'll work on setting up for you to meet the artists you've been dealing with at the gallery. Whole villages will be honored to meet you. Is it a plan?" Beth nodded.

They talked more about plans, dreams, and details of schedules until they parted with a long-held hug.

As Beth walked away, she thought how quickly things changed. She now held a job, career, and home, all at once. This windfall gave her the freedom to continue on her chosen path. She'd be losing the daily support of her best friend. Distance usually became an impediment to closeness. She knew they'd email, call and stay in touch, but it wouldn't be the same, not even with Facebook.

She leaned against the door of her car, crossed her arms across her chest, still trying to take in all that transpired this one afternoon. She looked at her shoes and the sidewalk, noticing the leaves, pebbles and debris at her feet. Her artist's eye caught the symmetry, textures and colors there. Time passed. She focused on a big, single water drop on her shoe. She looked up expecting to see rain falling, then comprehended the drop fell from her own eyes as huge tears coursed down her cheeks, dripping in perfect circles on the toes of her shoes. Not sure how long she'd been entranced, she hurriedly wiped her eyes. She'd not cried in a very long time, not through the worst of the physical beatings or emotional abuse from Marc, while living in the shelter, or through the divorce or the pressure of finishing her degree. Now, at the prospect of such sweeping changes, changes in some recent constants, ending some and beginning others, she found her previously lost ability to tear up and weep, whether from sadness or happiness, or both. Tears represented that she cared again, had a new capacity for deep feelings. She gave herself the important permission to mourn, acknowledging emotions once more. Maybe she was healing after all.

The days melted together. Guests at the special party following her graduation proved to be an eclectic mix of rich, poor, children, adults, socially adroit and new to socializing, side-by-side with creative artists. When her turn came to speak at the party, she looked around the room, acknowledging each one for the role they played in helping her arrive at this point. "I'm so honored for you to be here. It's a joy to me to see you smiling. Actually, it's overwhelming. Thank you so much. I made a little surprise for each of you, in gratitude for your friendship. It is a small token of appreciation for you, which is my custom at a time such as this, to honor you, my friends." She give each of them a handcrafted dream catcher, a small circular web made from bark, twigs and twine, shells, and stones, carefully woven, with a tag outlining the story of the spider. "Each one is different, just as each of you is different. Please accept my little giveaway. Symbolically, the web catches the bad dreams allowing only good dreams to filter through." She'd spent weeks making each of them, her good wishes and prayers going into each one individually.

Charlotte's caterers prepared several ethnic dishes for the buffet. Everyone enjoyed the huge bowls of salads, trays of meats, cheeses and breads. The kids thought they must be in heaven, eyeing the dessert tables loaded with pie, cakes, cookies and homemade candies. A big punch bowl, filled with red punch made from fresh strawberries and ice cream required refilling over and over. The decorations also gave the party a festive air, from the ice sculptures inlaid with wide-open roses, to the paper decorations made by the children, strung above their heads, waving in the air. An impromptu art show of the children's artwork magically emerged on one end of the room. Parents and benefactors alike marveled at the rag tag expedition of their art, each one exceptional in their childlike expression.

After the party, Beth moved into Charlotte and Eddie's now empty upstairs apartment. She set up the huge windows and tall ceilings of the back bedroom with lace curtains to keep it airy. Newly installed shelves and counters held supplies and a sink for easy cleanup. She brought in some comfy seating, stools for working and easels, along with her pottery wheel. She installed a kiln outside on the patio to fire her pottery. She loved the prospect of working on her craft there.

Her daily schedule called for her to roll out of bed in the morning, then go downstairs to oversee the gallery and sync schedules with the staff. She then lunched with clients, friends, or other artists.

Three days a week traveled to the shelter to hold art classes for kids. One night a week, she taught art classes with their moms, too. She didn't go out much the other nights, afraid to run into Marc or his family. She retreated to her own little studio to paint, craft or pot.

"Beth, you must let us hang your big paintings at the gallery. We'll schedule a special show. We can plan one in New York, too," Charlotte insisted.

"I don't know—that's a lot of work. What if no one likes it? Or worse, no one comes to the show?" A private show notoriously meant a lot of work and a certain amount of risk. Exciting as a solo showing might potentially be, it's also hard for an artist, especially a new one.

"You let me worry about that. I know my clients will love your stuff, Beth. Those huge canvasses of yours with all those dark emotions promise to be a big hit, I just know it."

"I created them just for my own catharsis, Charlotte—they're raw, too personal," she whined.

"Exactly. That's why they're so good. They contain meaning and truth. I'm telling you, girl, you ought to do this."

When Charlotte saw her post-Marc pottery pieces, she insisted that they be included in the gallery display, too. A few pieces of her work came to be added to one of the back rooms. She eventually developed a following of her own as her work started becoming popular, which pleased her. The money she earned through her work thrilled her, too.

Charlotte dragged her to a few parties, and these always proved beneficial to her, either from the exposure to other artists or potential donors to the shelter, or increased traffic into the gallery. Charlotte's unfailing eye to recognize opportunities started to rub off on her.

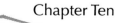

Chapter Ten

Charlotte's Shower

Beth decided to throw Charlotte with a baby shower before she left. Charlotte and Eddie's culture didn't have baby showers, where mothers invited friends to play baby games, drink tea and bring presents for the new baby. It caused quite a stir at the Embassy when word got out in town and back home in their country, also. Charlotte's sisters wanted to come over and her mother-in-law, Eddie's mother, also wanted to come. Since the current Queen wanted to travel to attend a simple baby shower, it gained grander proportions.

"I want to pay for the food, Beth, and the decorations, I insist," Eddie told her. "In fact, because you're so good to accommodate all my extra guests, let's move the whole event to that seafood restaurant Charlotte loves. You just leave those arrangements to me, okay?" he stated with authority.

"But Eddie ..."

"Now, Beth," he insisted, overriding her objections. Eddie insisted on buying the refreshments. He made arrangements to book the entire restaurant for the afternoon. Charlotte liked the little buttery biscuits they served, so Eddie insisted on ordering those along with heavy hors d'oeuvres for the party as well. Beth became a bit dismayed that their small little tea party baby shower was turning into an afternoon extravaganza—practically a state event. In view of Charlotte and Eddie's happiness, she didn't have the heart to back out.

The invitations looked like little diapers that opened up with the party particulars inside. The guest list, now over a hundred, included the wives of the diplomats throughout Central Africa, along with Charlotte's friends and Beth's colleagues, as well. Eddie turned over the event to the protocol staff of the Embassy. The checklist of duties grew proportionately with the guest list. She eventually turned over the seating and place cards to Eddie's staff. Beth thought they could forego the games, but no one would hear if it. If games occurred as entertainment at showers, then they wanted to do games. She gave up trying to organize the games, allowing the staff to organize that, too. They'd never played the "diaper the baby blindfolded relay" or listed baby names out of the words in a sentence, or passed the diaper after looking inside to name the kind of candy bar inside. Perhaps they could divide partygoers into smaller teams and still play the games.

"This event is shaping up to be quite a cosmopolitan party," observed Sharon, Beth's assistant. "We're blending of several cultures, partaking in a uniquely American activity."

"Native American women didn't tend to host the punch, cake and games kind of showers, either. They simply laid out a meal and opened the gifts. Different communities evidently produce different customs," Beth acknowledged.

Several days before the party, Charlotte's sisters, Emmie and Sylvie, hit town supposedly "to help." They ended up spending most of their time shopping, eating and nightclubbing. It boggled Beth's mind that people flew around the world to attend a baby shower, albeit a special one.

The day before the party, Eddie's mother, the current monarch, arrived in Washington. She set time aside to tour the gallery. Arriving in a sleek black limo, with flags on the front, Beth watched through the gallery window as Mrs. Ramalde stepped out. She held the regal bearing of a monarch. Taking the ornately carved cane given her, she came through the door, followed by Charlotte and Eddie, and then half a dozen others, a mix of aides and security personnel.

Short of stature, Mrs. Ramalde, known as Queen Nefier, wore close-cropped natural hair against her beautiful, smooth, dark skin. Her limb movements were graceful, and measured. Beth would describe her as elegant. Her sparkling eyes saw everything, while her stern countenance gave away nothing.

She wanted to see every piece as if to give her personal approval to each. Eddie walked with her as Charlotte came up behind. Beth stood ready to talk about each item. Beth felt Mrs. Ramalde tested her with each question. Her slight, queenly nod each time gave Beth the idea she'd passed muster.

As she made ready to leave, Mrs. Ramalde motioned Beth aside. They sat under the huge windows on comfortable couches, with a low table in front of them, covered in magazines. The others busied themselves elsewhere, pointedly looking away.

She instantly set Beth at ease. "I'm happy to meet you, Beth. I've heard how much you contributed to the success of this effort, which has meant so much to our people. You've also been a good friend to our dear Charlotte and my Eddie as well."

Beth eventually stammered a reply. "Charlotte and Eddie have been wonderful to me. They've helped me in so many ways. I dearly love them, as well."

Mrs. Ramalde smiled saying, "Then it is good. It is good of you to host this "shower" for them. I am told that it is not like a ceremony, and doesn't involve water. Tell me what to expect tomorrow."

"The baby shower is the event a woman's friends give her to celebrate the impending birth of her baby, to give her some items to use for the baby," Beth explained. "Usually, everyone gathers at someone's home or a restaurant or hall. Sometimes we play games with a new baby theme. Everyone gets to act silly, laughing with friends. Winners receive small prizes. I'm afraid that Charlotte's small shower has grown very large. We still want all the usual elements, but it's getting harder to keep that intimate feel. I'm trying to make everything especially nice for Charlotte. She's very happy that you can enjoy it with her."

"Thank you." Queen Nefier nodded thoughtfully. "I hope I'm not burdening you. Two more of my sisters arrive tomorrow for the event. I'd count it a personal favor if they could be seated."

It sounded more a command than a request. Clearly, Queen Nefier usually got her way. She got it now, too. "Two more ... of course, we'll take care of them," Beth said. She tried to imagine changing the seating yet again. "I'm amazed that Eddie's family traveled so far for this. How is it that they'd make such an effort to come to this little shower?"

The Queen smiled indulgently at Beth, saying, "As soon as they heard about Charlotte's American friend giving her an event in honor of our new heir, they insisted on coming here. We may want to start the new custom of showering the baby ourselves. I'm pleased you have been a friend to our whole country and to Charlotte especially. Edward came here to learn and to make connections advantageous to our country. He faces some strong challenges at home with reforms to be made and financial and diplomatic hurdles to overcome. I feared Charlotte would be too strong a distraction, keep him from focusing on his tasks. He has enjoyed his time here and accomplished much as a diplomat and facilitator, both of which he needs to engage on behalf of his country from here on. Charlotte, herself, has matured into a young matron, and this I think is due in large part to your influence. I bear a small token gift to you, a memento." She motioned for one of her aids to come forward with a small square box. "I hope you like it. It is native to my country, and women wear it as part of their ceremonial dress."

Beth opened the box finding a beautiful gold cuff bracelet, intricately made, with intertwining vines of raised and hammered design, about three inches wide. Several natural polished yellow stones were set among the gold leaves. Underneath lay a matching set of hair combs and earrings of the yellow stones. They would look spectacular in Beth's dark hair. Beth made a mental note to ask Charlotte to send more of this artists' work over here for the gallery.

"It's so beautiful. I love it. I'll treasure it always," she graciously thanked her. Beth's eyes started to tear. She dropped to her knees in front of Mrs. Ramalde to hug her in spontaneous thanks. Mrs. Ramalde, although not expecting a showing of affection, hugged Beth back. "I made you a little necklace as a greeting gift," said Beth. "It's made from local clay. I painted and fired it, the beads that is, and strung it for you. Let me get it." She ran out to the gallery desk, then back with a small gift-wrapped box.

Mrs. Ramalde opened it, held it up to admire it, and said, "It's truly lovely. That it is given by the artist is very special."

"It's our Native American custom to bring a greeting gift, a small token to honor a new relationship. This is my greeting gift to you. I am honored you accept my gift." They planted the seeds for a lasting relationship.

Mrs. Ramalde said, "We must leave now to go to a little party in our honor elsewhere. We will see more of each other tomorrow."

As the entourage left, Beth grasped that they were probably headed to the White House for a state dinner.

Beverly Waters McBride

 Chapter Eleven

D.C. Gallery/ Baby Shower

The morning of the shower, Beth ran down the stairs with her thermal coffee cup in hand to check on the multiple last-minute details. Everything should be ready; however, last minute problems invariably made everyone frantic. She stayed up late into the night to finish the last of the little macramé and bead bracelets she personally made for each of the guests. She attached her personal business card to bracelet, with a good wish for them on the back of each card, to go into "goodie bags" they'd assembled for each guest. She hoped they struck the right chord of playful, yet dignified.

Beth headed over to the restaurant first thing to check on the decorations and nametags. She then planned to come back to shower and dress for the 1:30 event. As hostess, she wanted to arrive back at the restaurant early to greet guests.

The banquet room had been transformed into a baby shower paradise. Streamers of beautiful pastel sheer fabric, strung from a four-foot hanging cherub in the center, turning in a circle, with a crystal chandelier hung in each corner of the room. Blue and yellow fabric with the mildest suggestion of pink, brought together everyone's fondest wish that the forthcoming heir would be male. Each table held multi-tiered floral arrangements of all roses: yellow, white, pink, red and even blue and green! The entire room was transformed into an indoor spring garden, with trellises, baskets of long, graceful gladioli, and pots of huge mums in every empty spot. All that lacked for this once bare, sterile restaurant banquet room to look like a garden was a rock fountain and gravel paths between the tables. At each place setting, a half-page vellum program with blue and yellow tassels and gold printing announced the order of the party. She hadn't expected a published order. This was supposed to be just a baby shower, after all, but it was too late now to object.

The diaper-shaped nametags and the goodie bags lay out along the table by the door. She checked with the buffet staff, satisfied with the food and drinks. The bakery arrived with the clever sleeping baby-shaped cake, and trays of blue cupcakes.

A gift table already held a few presents, elaborately

wrapped in the typical pastel colors and gauzy ribbons. A few packages arrived from Africa, too, covered in brown shipping paper.

The Embassy sent over a few extra helpers, servers and protocol experts to properly introduce each guest and so things would go smoothly for a room full of women, many of them strangers.

The obligatory reception line formed spontaneously, with Beth, Charlotte, and Eddie's mother, Queen Nefier. It went without a hitch—thanks to so many embassy staff hovering, it wouldn't dare go any other way. Beth found she already knew many of these women or heard of them through Charlotte.

Many of the guests arrived wearing eye-catching, elaborate native garb. Beth chose a flared white leather skirt, a loose brown shirt and a short white leather jacket with her chunky turquoise jewelry, happily retrieved from Marc's safe.

"Love your jewelry, Miss Beth," Charlotte commented.

"Why, thank you, Ms. Charlotte," Beth countered, "I owe it all to you, my darlin'." They laughed at their private joke.

Beth stayed near the front of the room as people arrived to help explain the penny game. Charlotte took to it right away, immediately drew and announced a penny from her treasure jar with a date of 1963. That date buzzed through the room as each guest looked at her own penny. A squeal erupted from the middle of the room as someone waved another penny in the air. The portable microphone was pressed into her hands for all to hear her association with Charlotte and her wish for the baby.

"My name is Sabile," the young woman spoke carefully in British-accented English, "I know Charlotte through my working with Prince Edward at the Embassy here. Princess Charlotte has been very, very kind to me, helping my family settle here and ensuring we were all happy in our work. My wish for this new baby is for him or her to be wise. He will be raised to be strong and smart and a good person, for that's his family's way. I know he will be loved by them and all of us." She gestured around the room as many present nodded in understanding and agreement. "I wish for him extra wisdom and discernment as he grows into his future, facing all that lies before him. Or her."

Sabile blushed, hanging her head, not wanting to show her emotions, as all in the room applauded her and Charlotte. Everyone then caught on to the penny game and thereafter, it became the hit of the party. All the partygoers wanted to be chosen to speak. Several gave quite moving impromptu speeches in response to Charlotte calling out penny dates throughout the party.

Next, they lined up into relay teams for the Dress-the-Baby-Blindfolded-Relay. Confusing at the start, when the whistle blew for the relay to begin, the shouting became deafening. Women directed others from the sidelines, cheering their teams. It reminded her of the antics at the polo games where the socialites made a big deal of replacing the divots in the grass on the field. These cosmopolitan women shouted out wrong advice to competitor teams, slipping off their fancy shoes to cross the finish line faster. Some laughed so hard, tears came to their eyes. They'd never done anything like this. Queen Nefier wanted to try and assumed her turn blindfolded. Her sisters, who Beth called "the aunts" proved to be gregarious women who traveled a great distance to be there, joked infectiously, and became involved in playing the boisterous games. They squealed, pointing and covering their mouths as they whispered to each other. Those two would be a lot of fun at an otherwise stuffy state event.

As Charlotte began opening the amassed gifts, Queen Nefier sought Beth out to thank her and praise the party.

"I can't remember when I've had more fun. We definitely must bring this custom to my country. I see how good it is to have an intimate party with sisters, cousins, and friends. Please, may I call you if we need help getting this going?

"Of course, you may. Just call me. Or Google baby showers, also."

"I've heard of Google. Do you think I could learn it? You recommend it?"

"I find it helpful, sometimes."

"Then I shall learn to Google, too. Thank you. No wonder Charlotte speaks so highly of you. I want to personally invite you to visit us and certainly when Edward is crowned. We would be honored to welcome you to our land. You may come at any time and be assured of a welcome. I'd like for you to meet my husband, Prince Edward's father. He would most certainly like to meet you, too. I would very much like to learn more about your native heritage. Charlotte has told me a bit about what she has learned from you. I am fascinated by the history of your native peoples."

Beth, rendered almost speechless again, was surprised that Queen Nefier expressed interest in her own tribal heritage. "Why, thank you, Queen Nefier, I am honored with your invitation. I'm curious about your country."

The aunts set off a bombshell in the room by offering $10 for the women's shelter to anyone who should trade them the handmade bracelets Beth made for the goody bags.

"We love these bracelets and wish to carry them home as gifts. We'll donate $10 each if you'll give us your bracelet." They appropriated the mike and the bargaining. The sales went fast and furious.

"Thank you ladies," Henrietta said in a voice loud enough all to hear. "We collected $550 for the shelter. We are rounding it up to one thousand dollars in honor of Charlotte, our beautiful niece and Beth, our beautiful hostess."

Beth decided to think about setting up a little cottage industry, teaching staff and women to make them for fundraisers. That would certainly be a lasting legacy. Maybe they could call them "Charlotte's Bracelets," in honor of all her support for women's services.

After the last present had been packed up for return to the Embassy and the last guest had said goodbye, Beth collapsed in a chair, kicking off her shoes. Thank goodness, someone else suffered the duties of cleaning up the decorations and washing the dishes, since they had made arrangements for the leftover food and flowers to go to the shelter.

Late that night at her home, Beth was overwhelmed by the urge to work. Eventually she became uneasy, as if someone watched her as she worked her pottery wheel. She looked out the window, seeing only the darkness outside. It was nothing to put her finger on, just a little nagging feeling.

When she finished the pot she worked on, she again made her way to the window, looking out into the night. She saw nothing out of the ordinary. Darkness shielded the street at that time of night, without a lot of traffic moving. Nothing looked out of order. She decided to call it a night.

Chapter Twelve

Maryville: Life as a Returning Yooper

Maryville in the Eastern Upper Peninsula of Michigan, known as Yooper country, enjoyed long, harsh winters followed by short summers every year. On the Canadian/U.S. border, Maryville included multiple cultures, all competing among the hardy populace. Beth observed that the activities of the town-and-gown folks from the University differed widely from those of the Tribal government and its people, while the town folk, who belonged to neither of those groups also had a completely divergent lifestyle. Yet they all lived, worked, shopped and played hockey side-by-side. She felt a kinship with all of them, and strong loyalty to the U.P. She relished the whole Yooper experience, too. Yoopers never let a little thing like a massive snowfall or sub-zero temperatures faze them either.

She was grateful that no one here knew about her growing reputation in the art world, at least the one developing on the lower East Atlantic Coast and in Europe. She also learned that some of her work had been exhibited as far away as Miami, Naples and Sanibel in South Florida. She'd love to go visit some of the galleries holding her work someday. However, that was a long way from Northern Michigan's Upper Peninsula, by anyone's reckoning. Few folks here knew about her MFA (Master of Fine Arts), the prominent showings and exhibits, many of which she attended in New York or Georgetown, or that she led quite a different life among the art set away from here. She kept all that tucked away. She vowed not to let her quasi-celeb status turn her own head either. "Just keeping it real," she often chuckled to herself.

Still in a small town, after all, gossip usually found its way around soon enough. What they didn't know already, they'd manufacture anyway. She admitted, perhaps she'd been a touch, shall we say smug, when she met Marc and they enjoyed their whirlwind courtship and storybook church wedding. She'd left town, going off to live a life of privilege elsewhere, although that didn't quite work out as had she envisioned, either. She'd left the flourishing gallery securely in the hands of Charlotte's sisters. She'd always wanted to return home to teach kids, so when things fell in place with the sisters, she made her graceful exit.

She knew her anonymity couldn't last forever, but for now, she'd keep her own counsel.

Beth refrained from flaunting her native heritage. Not always comfortable expressing her feelings about her identity, her sense of belonging in the community lagged, too. She noticed when people savored their native worth in big ways, like spending thousands of dollars and time on their dance regalia for pow-wow. She hoped her experience of her native heritage went beyond tobacco discounts for cigarettes or gasoline, or exclusively to pow-wows, in favor of learning her place in this world. However, she didn't speak the native language or know much about the impact of the past on the culture. She sometimes found her lack of knowledge frustrating. If she worked up the gumption to ask Big Man, the Shaman, maybe he'd help her find the right teacher.

Soon after arriving back into town one of her first tasks became unloading tools, supplies, and equipment necessary to set up a studio. No artist supply store selling the complexity or volume of art supplies she required existed conveniently around the corner in this small town. She must plan ahead, purchase her supply of paints, canvas, clay and drawing paper in bulk and then set up delivery or drive downstate to pick them up. To hold her supplies and create a workspace, she rented a large unit in a building on the river among the marine businesses and waterside storage. She hoped to purchase it eventually from the owner.

She told her mystified landlord, the all-business, no nonsense, Mr. Peck, why she chose his building for her studio. "I can go there, turn up the heat, open the huge rolling door, then paint and pot, listen to music and look out at the river at the Great Lakes ships passing by to my heart's content. Here, I don't worry about late hours, or making noise, or bothering people with my kiln or wheel or music. It's perfect for my purpose."

"Whatever floats your boat, young lady," the curmudgeonly elderly landlord replied. "I installed an alarm system, so it should be safe for you, if you're determined to spend time here. Don't forget you are the one paying the heating bill." That was as close as he usually came to a joke. She didn't mind paying that heating bill, although it cost a lot to heat it enough to habitat during those unusually cold winter days. She needed her space, though, and her freedom and safety.

Sometimes she felt strong, full of purpose, but at other times, her insides were like jelly, inconsistent, and certainly not powerful. With her artwork, she now chose whether to share, keep, destroy or display it. She didn't bother to correct anyone's perception that she was "just" a lounge waitress. That described her, yes. Yet, beyond that, she boasted a growing following in the art world. You couldn't tell by looking. So far, she'd only allowed a few pieces, the safe ones that mostly illustrated her innate sense of hope, to be seen by the public. She found she liked showing nature in different ways, revealing her way of seeing it.

She and Charlotte still spoke on the phone, e-mailed, and chatted and posted on Facebook. They each moved on, yes; however, the friendship bond remained and tugged on her lonely heart strings again. Charlotte complimented Beth often, insisting more of her work should be on display. She'd even professed to appreciate the dark paintings, the huge canvases she painted during her divorce that evoked so much emotion in the people Beth allowed to see them. Beth remembered how much she missed her dear friend, Charlotte.

When she first arrived back in town, Beth ran into Dan's twin sister, Melinda. Beth saw the surprise on her face before she covered it up. If encountering Beth threw her off momentarily, she recovered quickly. The narrow aisles at Super Val-u Grocery stood barely wide enough for two carts to pass. They stood talking in the more roomy vegetable section near the back.

"What are you doing here?" Melinda asked in a less than friendly tone, suspicious of Beth's return.

"I'm renting right now in the old Watson house, working evenings at the Casino."

"Hmmm," she said. "What brings you back?"

Beth hesitated, thinking what she should say. Right then they moved their carts to let another shopper through. When they wheeled their carts back together, Beth launched a different topic.

"Tell me how you're doing. How's the kids and Harry?

Melinda warmed to the topic, launched into a description of her kids, ending by saying of her husband, "Harry is just Harry."

The grocery store presented as good a spot as any to run into Melinda, since she spent time there often. Known for cooking for family, potlucks, fundraisers, and taking dishes to the sick and elderly, she may well be the Tasmanian Devil of community service, a whirlwind of activity. She balanced home, family and community in spectacular ways, and many people depended upon her. Beth marveled that she never tired of it or resented that people actually demanded more once a good deed occurred regularly for them. Melinda never failed to provide, seemingly on a mission to feed others.

"I'm making a big dish of scalloped potatoes for the potluck at the Culture Center tomorrow. Did you hear about Auntie Casey being sick? I'm taking over some dishes for their dinner, too.

"That's good of you, Melinda. I'm sure they appreciate it," she reinforced. She hesitated, then asked, "What do you hear from Dan?"

Up the Creek

Everybody knew if anyone kept tabs on Dan, it was Melinda. Getting any information though, usually required listening to some elaborate yarns and stories about his exploits. Beth wanted to convey only a polite curiosity.

Melinda's facial expression turned blank. Beth waited, tension rising as Melinda's body stiffened. She tossed a bag of potatoes off the nearby shelf into her cart before she reluctantly replied.

"He's out of the country right now. He travels all over the world and is gone from here quite a bit. He works with some very interesting people. I understand he's sought after. Imagine our Dan socializing with the jet set? He's a carefree bachelor."

"I see," Beth said, hiding her disappointment. Struggling to keep her composure, she croaked out, "I'm really very happy for him." Uncomfortable, she mumbled a hasty goodbye. "I really gotta to run, so … "

After they parted, Beth left the few items in her cart, exploding out of the store to the safety of her car.

She sat there, head down on the wheel of her small car, trying for some equilibrium, her heart pounding, eyes burning. It hurt to learn that he lived away now, having fun, adventures, seeing other people, and probably other women. Perhaps she'd been naïve.

She decided to go to her studio for a while to sublimate out all this relationship angst on the pottery wheel. She often focused on working, sitting for hours producing pot after pot, vase after vase. Sometimes in the midst of emotional throes, she produced her best work.

Chapter Thirteen

Maryville: Redoux

"Marty, please make that two tequila sunrises, a pina colada, two margaritas, one tequila straight, and one house draft." Beth sounded out her order to Marty, working behind the casino lounge bar. She was back in Maryville, working as a waitress at the casino lounge, just like before she left four years ago.

Typical of lounges, the casino lounge held an array of liquor bottles displayed behind a room-long upholstered bar, with kitschy neon beer signs for decoration. Plush dark upholstered booths lined the room on three sides, with tabletop to ceiling glass bricks instead of walls. Not exactly a dive, yet not so fancy either, she thought. The room buzzed this typical Friday night with patrons at most every booth and chair, enjoying their libations and conversations.

"So Marty, where's my next order?"

"Right here waiting for you, doll." Like a dancer behind the bar, never wasting a motion, he reached for the right glass, poured the required ingredients and deposited the perfect drink on her waiting tray. Not the typical bartender, he was smart, funny and totally drama-less. He possessed an exceptional memory. She had befriended him when she worked the casino lounge before, then again when she came back to work here a few months ago. They greeted each other like old friends. Marty maintained a trim, strong physique, the better to lift heavy liquor cases, which showcased his short-clipped dark hair, and sparkling dark eyes. A master at getting others to confide about themselves, he was known as a good bartender, ready to pour another drink, encouraging his patrons to talk. Although friends for years, Beth nevertheless wasn't sure about his personal circumstances, whether he had a girlfriend or even a boyfriend, for he always deflected questions, even direct ones. He joked with the waitresses and customers, kept to himself, and was always on time and never out sick, which is an employer's dream.

She worked her preferred shift until 2:00 A.M. She liked working nights, prime tipping time in the beverage-serving world. So far, she'd not told anyone else here about her accomplishments or experiences in the art world. For that matter, she hadn't told them about any of her life. No sense dredging up the old hurts, like her sadness during her marriage or the disappointment of living with her elderly aunt or the discrimination she experienced as a Native American growing up.

Marty knew a little, as she'd confided in him somewhat. She thought her life was pretty much like everyone else's, good and bad, with ups and downs. At one time, she considered herself an open book, transparent for all to see. Now, with the recent divorce and trauma, that book remained closed. She'd choose when and who became privy to her life.

This little foray back into the waitressing world felt like a redo. Back home now felt less like coming home to lick her wounds, more like returning to look for a good emotional and mental footing. While she'd not yet achieved her peace, there remained hope.

Balancing her tray, she padded back to deliver their order to the six rowdy girls in the back booth. They had burst into the lounge a few minutes ago, noisy, just short of obnoxious, dressed in exaggerated glitter: casual, overly sparkly and jingly, in their too tight skinny jeans, too high heels and too low-cut tops. Beth recognized this must be one of their rare "girls night out" treats. Before walking next door to the casino theatre to see their heartthrob, a one-night traveling performance of a once-famous, now aging rocker, they gossiped and teased each other, making ribald or sometimes catty remarks. Beth slowed to listen as she cleared empties from their table, in anticipation of the next round. They reminded her of herself, not so many years ago. Even the conversation sounded familiar.

"So, Martha, how long to pour you into those jeans, girl?"

"About as long as you needed to trowel on that face, Jeannie." They all howled with laughter and toasted each other. Beth shook her head and took their order for another round.

Friday and Saturday nights bought out groups of friends to enjoy their evening at the casino or more often, rue their losses, since the house always wins. She actually enjoyed helping their evening along, feeling a sort of vicarious participation in their fun. Her job amounted to helping turn time backwards for them to act like carefree and rambunctious girls for this one night. She wasn't concerned about contributing to their drinking, since she knew these women carried their responsibilities very seriously. She knew, while husbands, boyfriends, kids and jobs came first, they enjoyed their infrequent nights out. She raised the heavy tray precariously to her shoulder, slapped on a smile and made her way over to the table to sort out the ordered drinks.

With any luck, she'd only be doing this a few more months until a teaching job opened up at one of the schools.

"You need to be doing something other than spending the best night hours in this bar," Marty told her more than once. "You possess a way out of here, an education. You need to move on." She knew he said it out of concern. She fluffed it off, as usual.

"I know, Marty, but I'd miss joking around with you too much to let go of all this glory," she joked, gesturing around the alternately gloomy, garish atmosphere of the lounge. He shook his head and plunked her order on her tray. She knew he'd say it again on another day, too, until she actually moved on for something better.

"Besides," she added, "I need to stay busy; otherwise, I'd find some trouble." She didn't like the idea of living off her savings from her divorce settlement or gallery sales. She never enjoyed sitting back idle, even in the worst of times.

Her straight-ahead stare returned to the reality of standing barside, yet again. The constant cha-ching, the din of conversation and occasional shouts of winners returned.

Waiting for her order to come up, a vaguely familiar person passing by the lounge caught her eye. There walked Dan Walkin, her ex-boyfriend, lover, confidant, nemesis, all rolled into one still remarkably attractive package. She quickly looked away, then could not resist darting her eyes back toward him, observing him from the darkened confines of the lounge without discovery. His looks caused her breath to catch, even after all these years.

He looked the same. No, slightly older, more subdued, walking with the cocky self-assurance she remembered from their childhood. He seemed more self-assured, and if possible, more in control. Nicer clothing now, with styled haircut and oh-so tight jeans. His manner had always drawn her to him. Even at age nine, playing on the school playground, something about him entranced her.

He stopped to greet friends she didn't know. She watched as they shook hands, slapped backs and spoke softly. Together, they turned toward the lounge, heading to the entrance. Oh, please let him walk on by. In he walked, living and breathing, among his friends, then sat down in <u>her</u> lounge.

The back booth girls walked by her standing there, wishing her a good night, as they headed for the show next door. For a moment, she wished she could go with them, if only to keep from facing Dan.

This must be her day of reckoning. Crap! Of course, his little entourage headed for one of her booths. Naturally!

Mustering up her courage, she marched over to his booth to secure their order.

"What'll you have, folks?" she said with a brightness she didn't feel. She saw immediately that he recognized her voice. His body stiffened, his head pivoted to her direction. Her face drained as his turned bright red. Neither spoke for a moment. The couple with him saw it and waited while she and Dan tried to recover.

"I'll take just orange juice, thank you," he said softly, watching for her reaction. She gave none. She took their orders, a house draft and a seven and seven. As she turned away to leave, he grabbed her hand and held it. Something like a lightning bolt struck when they touched. Again, Crap!

"Can you spare a few extra orange slices with that?" he asked her. He only wanted extra orange slices for his drink.

"Sure, I'll take care of it," she said, relieved, before making a hasty retreat back to the safety of the bar. Only then did she breathe again.

"You OK, honey?" asked Marty. Beth nodded once. "If you want me to serve your order, I will and I'll even give you the tip," he said conspiratorially, winking.

Beth shook her head. Dammed if she'd let Dan think he affected her. Not in this lifetime!

After delivering their order, she made a quick getaway escaping to stand outside in the chilly night on her seldom-used break time. The other waitresses would be thrilled for the extra tips for a little while tonight.

Later he sought her out, came over to speak with her, and then asked her to meet him later to talk over old times. She reluctantly agreed, but had no expectations other than old friends catching up.

They caught up all right! Being around him brought back old feelings. It seemed easy to just let go and let her body respond. She felt all the relief and passion in her coming to the surface again. Although she wasn't ready to throw it all in just to be with him again just yet, it felt great to be around Dan again. He left town soon after for a job and she didn't see him for a while. It's just as well, she thought. Time alone would tell where this rekindling might go.

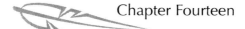

Chapter Fourteen

Maryville: Achieving Goals

"Well, Ms. Morrison, your application is all here, your transcripts and references look fine. You passed all your personal interviews. Now all that's left is for us to receive your certification from Lansing, then an opening in your field to occur here," said Ms. Fauls, who handled hiring and certification issues for the school district. As the staff person who'd set up Beth's interviews at the schools and assembled her credentials, Mrs. Fauls emerged as pivotal, like a personal lifeline, in Beth's long-range plan to be a teacher in Maryville. "You'll remember, I explained when we started your application that our school system doesn't produce a lot of openings year-to-year," Mrs. Fauls reiterated as Beth nodded. "It may be a while before your particular expertise is needed. It helps that you're available for both elementary and secondary. Your specialty is one unfortunately that is cut during a tough economy like now. Art education, just like music and the other enrichment subjects suffer first. If you're willing to accept Special Ed or something else to start, your chances might be somewhat better."

"No, thank you for asking though, Mrs. Fauls," Beth said without hesitation, "I think I'd rather hold out for art ed. I'm working elsewhere for now, so I'd appreciate you letting me know if any opening occurs. If we can work together like that, it may turn out best for all of us. I'm available days for substituting in art classes, also."

"Have you met Mr. Warren, our current art teacher?" Mrs. Fauls inquired. "He started with us two years ago. He keeps busy with traveling art classes at the three elementary schools and the middle school. Mrs. Morgan, whom you already met, handles the art department duties at the board and also teaches at high school. We're a small district, so everyone has double duty. Mr. Warren has been out ill a bit this year," she hesitated, "so we may need that substitute availability you offer." She looked at Beth meaningfully, as if she wanted to say much more. Beth filed it away without comment.

"I know it's none of my business," Mrs. Fauls whispered low, looking around to see who might be in the hallway, for discussing another school system would be frowned upon in her office, "but did you apply at the Tribal School or at Tribal Youth

Ed? I believe the Tribe has extra grants or programs from time-to-time."

"Yes, I applied both places. Same thing there, no openings at this time."

"It's great you're making the most of your options, Mrs. Morrison. May I call you Beth?" Beth nodded, appreciating her help.

"Please. I'd love you to."

"I'm sure we'll be calling on you whenever needed." she assured, standing up, the standard signal to leave.

Beth left the district office feeling brighter, a little bounce in her walk. She'd made a tiny step closer toward her goal. Now to wait. Teachers are needed everywhere, especially good ones, heaven knows. The State Office wouldn't hold up issuing her certification. The already filled art specialist position here in the school system remained the only hold up. She became intrigued by Mrs. Fauls' cryptic look about this Mr. Warren, the current person in the job.

When she'd met Mr. Warren, he appeared to have a lot going on, although not overly involved in the children's artwork. He hadn't been particularly friendly toward her at their brief meeting. In fact, he seemed surprised by her and looked at her strangely. Maybe he knew she wanted to be on a wait list for his job. She would ask around town about the situation. Surely someone would know something. She just needed to reach the right person who knew all the right gossip.

Maybe she'd best be open to other options, too. Perhaps encouraging and supporting tribal children would be something she should seriously consider. Mrs. Fauls suggested looking into the Tribal school. They said they couldn't hire at this time, but hoped to add some classes next year. It all would be decided over the summer, based on anticipated enrollment, and the number of current teachers who would be returning.

She visited the art classroom in the newly built tribal school, happening across some wonderfully creative projects under construction. No students worked in the room at the moment. She would love to see them working. Just looking around made her crave getting into the classroom setting again. Since she didn't think she'd appreciate someone nosing around in her classroom, she walked out into the hallway. Ojibway language word cards hung posted up high along the hallways. In the library, colorful cardboard village dioramas on display depicted a typical historical village in each season—summer, fall, winter and spring—featuring activities taking place in village life each season. The librarian showed her the students' projects. "This is a special project of our fifth graders," the earnest woman explained. "All the teachers make efforts to bring a Native American twist to their lessons, even math, history or science. The students researched and then built all these intricate village scenes," she said proudly. Beth couldn't help thinking wistfully it would be nice to be part of such a creative staff.

Later that day at Wal-Mart, she ran into the man she recognized as Barry Warren, the public school art teacher.

"You're Beth Morrison, aren't you?" he asked.

"You're Barry Warren, right?"

"Yes." He answered dismissively. "Join me for coffee in the snack bar other there," he invited, actually more like commanded. She went along with it.

"Sure," she replied, matching his demand with her good manners, as they moved to an empty table. They sat in the noisy table area where shoppers drank coffee and ate hot dogs or pretzels while they rested from bargain hunting. It served as a social gathering place in their community.

He asked her questions about her training and knowledge of artistic styles, but didn't really listen to her answers. Close to her own age, he had stocky build, with dark eyes covered by thick glasses. He told her he'd moved here from Wisconsin several years ago. His untidy, prematurely graying hair stood out around his square face. His eyes moved constantly, making people he spoke to want to follow his moving focus wherever he looked. It was very distracting, making her jittery.

He seemed somehow familiar, although she couldn't place him. Something about him felt off. He never smiled. His conversation alternated from polite to pointed so quickly that Beth questioned whether he liked her at all.

She asked him about his own philosophy of teaching, hoping to learn from an experienced teacher.

"Some of these kids never learn, they'll just waste supplies," he said, an arrogant sneer on his face. "These kids suck all the energy out of you."

"What do you mean, Barry?" she asked, wanting to hear why he thought that way.

"This town, these kids, they're just not destined to be artists. Unlike a true artist, they close off their creativity. Half of them wouldn't know art if it bit them on the butt. I've given them chance after chance to prove themselves worthy, but it's beyond them," he spat out angrily. Scared a little by the intensity of his opinion, she called him on it.

"You really don't mean that, do you, Barry? How can you assume they'll never produce? You allow them to grow, hope eventually they excel, and then praise their efforts," she said, putting forth her own ideas.

"You really are the Pollyanna, aren't you?" he said, a sneer creeping over his face, nose wrinkling. "You are definitely new at this. Take a word of advice, don't get all wrapped up in these kids. They're a void, believe me." His eyes bored into her with such intensity that Beth looked away, uncomfortable. After impaling her with a hard look, he pursed his lips, then looked as if he'd said too much. His hard gaze with narrowed eyes and taunt mouth in a pained expression would strike her funny if he wasn't, ludicrously, perfectly serious.

"I guess I need to finish my shopping," she stammered, looking around uncomfortably. They parted.

"Good luck finding a job, Beth, and keeping your soul intact," he said in such a way that Beth didn't believe he meant it. That sounded ominous. She became concerned for his students. "That guy's a nut case," she muttered under her breath. If he thought that way, why did he teach at all?

She shook her head, buried her thoughts and then became absorbed with her shopping.

Beverly Waters McBride

Chapter Fifteen

Detroit Connection

Several days later, Beth picked up the jingling cell phone with her usual cheerful "Hello?"

"Hello, is this Beth? This is your Aunt Bernadette from Detroit. I know we haven't spoken in a long time. I'm really sorry for that. I need to talk to you about your mama and daddy a little bit."

Beth sat down for this. She hadn't heard from anyone in her family in almost twenty years.

"How did you find this number? Aunt Bernadette, you say? I remember a Birdie, is that you?"

"Yes, that's me. I'm pleased you remember me at all. You were pretty young. I hated that business of having to send you up there to stay with Aunt El all by yourself. At the time, it seemed like the best solution. Hard times befell all of us. I couldn't bring you in as I just scraped by, myself. We wanted you to have a better chance than we thought you'd get in the foster homes down here.

Just today, I found your number from the white pages on the computer. First, I called a number in Maryland. They said you weren't there anymore, and were none too nice about it either, so I tracked you down to Maryville again."

"Oh," Beth said, letting it drop. Then her curiosity grew. "What did you want to talk about Aunt Birdie? A lot of time has gone by. I've pretty much made peace with my family not wanting anymore to do with me." She couldn't keep the sharp edge out of her voice.

"Oh, darlin', I'm so sorry to have left you for so long. I just didn't think that no one else would be looking in on you or keeping up with you, especially after Aunt El died. I feel so bad for not following up. I apologize. We've all got a powerful lot of apologizing to you." She paused for a moment. The dead air between them seemed like a stagnant, stifling, sick-making, holding of breath. "I'm calling for your mama. She was afraid to call you herself. She's been working on her twelve-step program for recovery for a while. She's all clean and sober now. She wants to make amends to you before anything else happens. Unfortunately, she's very sick now. She's in bad shape. She is ashamed for what happened to you, has a lot of regrets for a long time. The drink and drugs took over for many years. All that old history is causing her considerable pain. She wants more than to just cry and fret about you. She wants to ask you to forgive her. She could speak to you on the phone.

She's not able to travel right now or she'd make the trip up there to see you in person. Is there any way you could see your way clear to speak to her? It would mean the world to her. I'm not condoning what she done, I'm just trying to help my sister out, now that she's trying to help herself."

"Aunt Birdie, I'm going to have to think about this. I'm kinda not willing to just open the floodgates, forgive all and rush to her side. I've lived without a mother's love for too many years. I carry a good bit of anger and sadness about all of this. You and she will just need to understand that," said Beth, stating her case dispassionately.

"I do understand. I don't blame you one bit. My only concern is that time is running out for her and for you where she's concerned. I'd love nothing more than for her to find a little bit of peace where you're concerned before she goes. I also understand that we, as your family, have failed you. Forgiveness is not easy. I also believe that anger is going to help no one either. I'm asking you to think about it. Get back to me. It would mean a lot to all of us to make this right. Would you think about it, Butterfly girl?"

Butterfly girl. No one called her Butterfly girl for years. It struck a chord with her, a painful one. She'd kept that in her heart since a child and built tall fences around it for a long, long time. Her mother and Aunt Birdie used to call her Butterfly Girl. She didn't realize until right now that she avoided any butterfly motif work in her art. In fact, she took great pains to keep that theme out.

She would ponder the idea of being asked to rescue her mother at this late date. Why should she help her? Was it up to her to forgive now? She never asked for this new complication. She never considered being embraced back into the family tree. She had been just a child, hadn't asked to be rejected. She didn't know any of these people. Did she really owe them anything at all? They hadn't wanted her in their circle before now. Why now, just to ease the conscience of her ailing mother after all these years? Not her problem.

Her thinking went on the rest of the day along these lines—on one hand not wanting to accommodate their issues, while on the other fantasizing about nearly forgotten cousins, aunties, uncles—a whole family she never knew. A familiar yearning ground away in her midsection, as her emotions turned like an oscillating fan, first away from family and then towards them

That night she went to her studio, music blasting behind her. She'd been pulled toward some already prepared canvases. She toweled green in all the corners, layers of green hues to give the depth she wanted and then added some yellows she'd flesh out later. She mixed up an array of reds, oranges, magentas, and chartreuses. She wanted to throw them on the canvas to work out some of her anger. She dabbed in a little black and brown to reflect her sadness. Her optimism wouldn't let her mute the bright pinks she used, despite defiantly clinging to old feelings. She worked quickly, then stood back to stare at the product of the emotions surging inside herself. Not surprising, she identified a butterfly emerging from the cocoon on the left side, and another on the bottom right, as if ready to fly away. That was enough for now.

Her creation could rest, then later she'd define the two butterflies and the background a bit. Looking back, she followed the progression of the life cycle, showing the life of the butterfly first born, flight, and then completing the cycle. The deep vibrancy of her color choices surprised her. She evidently needed to grow to this point, to this release. She grew, just like the butterfly, to more peace within herself. She also wished peace for others, at least on the surface level.

She doubted these new family members were interested in her beyond that level. They may well think differently, but she owed them nothing. At the first bite from any of them, she could withdraw her extended hand, then be done with them all. She'd think about it though, before committing to some strained, emotionally wringing contact.

She called in sick the next day for work at the Casino. She rarely missed many days on the schedule. She spent the rest of the night sketching butterflies, feeling raw emotionally. She wanted them out of her system, and they wanted to come out. She worked feverishly in every medium. She cut clay into raised shapes for the pottery, which actually turned out beautifully. She drew with her pastels until her sensibilities told her to bring some new colors. The marketer in her thought some of these ought to go out into her next portfolio. She'd situate them on the shelf for now.

Chapter Sixteen

Maryville: Good Advice

Beth had thought about going to see Big Man, the Shaman, for a long time, but she didn't want to impose on him. She remembered hearing his family members relate horror stories about how many times thoughtless people presumed too much, insinuating themselves into his home or his schedule. Some people persisted in the idea that the Shaman ought to be available at their personal convenience. However, he needed some private time with his family, too. Sensitive to those stories and not wanting to intrude, she watched him from afar at pow-wows, spiritual gatherings, potlucks or ceremonies, treasuring a random nod or smile from him.

Actually, he was always open to people and generous with his time. He didn't call himself a shaman. He told people he was just learning to be Anishnabe. He said it takes a lifetime to be

Anishnabe. Others said he strove to stay true to his spiritual gifts, walking the narrow, sometimes difficult life path called the "red road." She had been told that sometimes his scrutiny made others uncomfortable, for he saw through people's masks, their illusions and behavior, good or bad. He cut to the core of their intentions with just a few well-placed words. He, of course, over time noticed her hanging back, but contrary to popular belief, he didn't presume to read her mind. He merely waited for her to come forward, while she waited for the perfect time. As a result, they hadn't yet talked.

Today, she happened to be alone, early in the afternoon, in the huge kitchen at the Cultural Building. She cooked soup and baked casseroles for a fundraiser dinner in honor of the Hawkins' family who traveled to Ann Arbor Hospital with their ill baby. Later, others would bring desserts, more potluck dishes that everyone would enjoy. They'd hold a 50/50 raffle for the family.

Snow fell outside, and the wind swirled around the growing drifts. The day was one of those dark, piercing cold, foreboding weather days, difficult be outdoors for very long, with no letup in the steady falling snow. Folks coming inside during the winter usually knocked the snow off outside the door, then hung their damp coats, hats and scarves inside, careful not to leave wet or salty tracks indoors.

Up the Creek

Big Man came into the building, having been dropped off early for the next meeting he would attend that afternoon. He often received tobacco to ask him to say a blessing or an opening prayer or a few inspiring words at the start of a gathering, as tonight at this dinner. At the door, he wiped his feet noisily on the mat, gave a polite shout that echoed in the huge empty room to let any people there know he'd arrived. Beth shouted back from the kitchen, acknowledging his presence, then continued cutting vegetables.

The cheery fire from the free-standing fireplace in the front of the open meeting room, stacked logs at the ready, radiated friendly warmth to eliminate some chill off the room. He salted the icy entrance steps from the bag of salt by the door, and added a few logs to the glowing embers. He sniffed the air and grinned, as the heady, full-bodied smells of food cooking in the massive kitchen wafted out to the bigger room with the promise of a plentiful dinner to come. He looked around to be sure he wouldn't be intruding on any meeting or gathering.

"My ride dropped me off early. Do you got any coffee goin'?" he asked her from the kitchen doorway, like a little kid with his favorite cup in hand and apologetic grin on his deeply lined face.

"You know I do," she replied. "Just sit right down there at the table and I'll get you some." She pointed him toward the long, paper-covered table set up for the meal later. He walked over, his scuffed boots dragging the floor, pulled out a metal chair, sat down with a sigh, and stretched out long legs under the table, his thumbs hanging from the belt loops of his jeans, hanging his frayed red baseball cap over his knee. His wore a thick, well-worn flannel, buttoned up shirt, layered over a much-washed t-shirt, long faded jeans bunching over his boots. His salt-and-pepper braid of thin hair, bound with a simple band, draped over his shoulder. His lined, deep-brown complexion, high cheekbones, proud nose and dark sparking eyes actually hid his age—fifties or his eighties—it would be hard to guess. He never said. He kept a busy schedule of meetings and events that would tire even a much younger man.

"Sit down and keep me company," he offered to her, grinning. His lean body curled into the chair, while his gnarled, thick hands cradled the now warm coffee cup. He pushed back the chair opposite him with his booted foot. She smiled with pleasure at his invitation, running to retrieve her cold Mountain Dew pop from the kitchen. After teasing about her choice for ingesting caffeine, as he gripped his second coffee, they sat in companionable silence for a while.

Finally, he stretched his arms over his head, asking her, "How do you like living back here?"

"I like it pretty well," she responded cautiously at first, then warmed up to the topic. "I've experienced some very good and some very bad times over the last few years. I wanted to return here to find some of the happiness from before, to take an emotional break from stress, and also return to my creative roots." Even to her own ear, her explanation seemed self-righteous.

He nodded, then asked her perceptively, "You think your happiness came from this location?" No one had asked her that before. He might as well have hit her between the eyes, driving home the fallacy of her thinking up to now. She stammered in recognition of the revelation.

"I thought so, up to right now when you ask me," she answered, defensiveness creeping into her voice, despite her best efforts to keep it light. Her mind leapt to run down the list of her actions over recent years, but every rationale she came up with sounded weak.

While her mind raced through a litany of truths and falsehoods she'd come to accept as her own, her eyes darted back and forth, up and down, a neurolinguistics field day.

"No one, no thing or no place is going to give you your happiness," he observed casually. "When you achieve your balance, your happiness, sadness, anger and fear will all balance. Then you will be at one with Creator, at peace with yourself."

She could weep. He looked unaware he'd just turned her thinking upside down. He summed up all her questions, all her doubts and guilt in two sentences in the space of five minutes. He propelled her quickly to ponder, understand and then forgive. Wisdom had been imparted to her at lightning speed. Why hadn't she sought him out before, trusting his answers for her? Grateful, she almost forgot to kick herself for being so dense. People sought him out for counsel for this very reason. He looked far over her head, to somewhere else for the moment, blinking without speaking, staring, yet not seeing. Finally he spoke, in a kind of sing-song, distant, disembodied voice. "I see it is a good thing you're here, for a healing. You have a mission especially with the babies, the binojii, the young ones. You are going to use those bad times to help many, many others. Many of The People will be helped by what you carry out, what you bring. Things are unfolding even now. You have new choices to make. Sadness from the past can be overcome, if you wish it so. You always think of others, and it is good, so you can expect opportunities to help others make things right. It is your choice whether to turn your childhood fears around and to forgive. You need to be cautious, not afraid. You are protected by very powerful spirit beings, who seek only good for you and The People."

He changed his focus then, taking a swig of his coffee. He gave her a big, toothy smile of satisfaction over his coffee cup, looking her straight in the eye, as if he knew a lot more. He kept it to himself, for now, seeming to realize instinctively how much she could take in.

She went to her purse bringing back a new pack of cigarettes to offer tobacco to her elder, according to their custom. She pushed them across the table to him with an inquisitive look.

He took the offered tobacco, thanked her and slid them in his shirt pocket with a nod.

Just then the door opened. Another cook arrived, making several trips to bring in more groceries. Other people soon came, each getting caught up in other conversations. She didn't speak to him again until after the meal, when he motioned her to come over to him as she walked by.

"I'm going to be over at the arena next Wednesday. Can you stop by? I'd like to tell you a few more things."

"I'd be honored to meet you there. I'll be excited to hear all you wish tell me. Can I bring you anything or bring something for you?"

"No, just you," he said, a man of few words.

When she met Big Man at the arena the next week, she found he had made arrangements for her to go to a sweat lodge for women and to the Women's Gathering. Her elder friend and art mentor, Ruth, would be going with her the Sugar Island Culture Camp for the Women's Gathering.

"You'll need to be open to some revelations and people from these two events," he told her, "and you drive Ruth to the meeting. You have some unfinished business from the past, eh?" he asked her. "Something from long ago needs to be resolved. It's up to you, as you alone have the power to finish it now. Does this make any sense to you?"

She gulped, then stumbled out a soft, "Yes, I understand." He alluded to her family and rotten childhood or perhaps her long past time with Dan or even with Marc. She dreaded to even think about those times again, much less make new decisions about them. Now she'd face doing something about her mother. She'd wanted to avoid that, and here it presented itself again, hitting her from another plane. She didn't want to dredge up her vulnerability all over again. She hesitated to open that door, lest her long lost family demand more out of her. She needed to think this through before taking any action, although she knew dealing with those old issues stood in the path to peace for her future.

He shrugged. "You know what's right," he said. He moved on to other thoughts, other issues.

Chapter Seventeen

Maryville: Quiet, Whimsical, Magical Buttercups

Beth drove her car around the edges of town, looking for a location to spend some time alone—somewhere undeveloped, with a view of the river. She wanted to be outside among nature, with "Mother Earth." She suffered spring fever, that phenomenon that strikes people who live in the far north during April as the snow melts and the sun warms the ground. Like everyone else, she experienced the persistent pull toward getting outside in the sunshine among the green stuff to feel some natural warmth on her skin. She wanted to suspend thinking for a while, allowing her mind to wonder, to let go of stressors, breathe deeply the cool damp air and pull in the scent of spring.

The vine-covered trees along the river road, aptly named Bayshore Drive, created a green canopy above her, with bright rays of sun shining through to beckon her into some mystical-like portal. In the countryside, interspersed with cabins, fishing homes, still closed-up summer residents' homes and a few die-hard year-round residents were occasional undeveloped fields. Her car moved along the twists and turns of the paved, potholed road, jolting with every frequent dip, typical of a post winter, northern country road.

She spotted the perfect location to sprawl out, an open field on the river's edge, bordered with tall trees and a welcoming carpet of new green grass. She backed the car up to study it for a few moments from afar as it formed a beautiful natural tableau, with hundreds of bright yellow buttercups waving low in the soft spring breeze. She loved being so close to the river, watching the big Great Lakes ships sliding quietly down the narrow river channel, to and from the Maryville locks. Canada loomed just across the river, similarly clad in residential homes and condos, but more densely developed.

She watched and listened from her car, waiting to see if it called to her. The field, blanketed with golden yellow flowers, gently rippling in the spring breeze indeed called her to skip to those flowers and lie down, roll around, and feel as one of them, with only her eyes and the top of her head sticking out. Relishing the dark green stems, leaves meeting the heads of cheerful yellow petals, buttercups happened to be her favorite wildflower. They evoked the memories of earlier short northern summers, flourishing under a uniquely UP sky, a background canvas of varied blue punctuated with small white clouds.

She stepped out of her car with just her sketchpad and charcoals, then reached back for her pastels at the last minute. Never sure what form inspiration might present, she liked being prepared for anything.

Despite her first inclination to rampage willy-nilly through the lush array of yellow flower tops, she picked her way among them instead, careful not to disturb the magic.

She sat on the ground, surrounded by gently waving buttercups. Looking closer, she discovered other small flowers, tiny white trillions, which abounded low to the ground. Inspired, she sketched a bit, working on getting down on paper some interesting geometric shapes that caught her eye. As her concentration moved away to the rolling currents of the nearby river, her eyes became heavy. She closed them, just to rest for a moment. She thought she heard someone call her name. She roused, eyes popping open, looking around, wondering who knew she was there. "Hello?" she said aloud. She heard no answer, saw only the rustle of nearby trees and the sensation of soft breeze cooling her body. Those quaking aspen trees can be quite noisy, she recalled, settling back into rest.

Awhile later, she heard her name again. This time

she kept her eyes closed, just listened, and waited. She held a stem of buttercup aloft, spinning it slowly. She looked through eyes slits, unfocused at the intense colors, shapes and texture of the little flower, staring at the perfectly formed petals, tiny veins, and deep yellow color around a center of delicate eyelashes. Twirling it left and right, she sensed a subtle change in the sounds around her, not alarming, just different.

As if someone spoke beside her ear, not like a speaking voice exactly, more like a "knowing." She saw, yet did not "see" defined shapes or forms. She comprehended on some level that she was having a vision. She wanted to remain open to the experience. She experienced anxiousness and exhilaration at the same time, with a comforting summation of her intentions, receiving approval for her good, positive spirit. She sensed relief and reinforcement down deep inside, to her very core. She affirmed choices she'd made, the rightness of creativity inside her, and forgiveness for mistakes. Mysteriously, like a healing, anger and sadness lifted away, while a sense of peace slid into and filled in around the dark corners inside her soul, rounding out still rough, frayed edges. Afterwards, she slept.

She later roused, stretching, feeling great. Birds still flew overhead, their calls breaking the silence, bringing her slowly awake. Her surroundings hadn't changed—she still lay among the simple, beautiful flowers, still sensing the sharp contrasts of the crisp spring day. She felt reluctant to leave her euphoric place or disturb the balance.

As if something important happened, grateful to have been privy to a special healing, a healing of her identity and of her soul, she would go away changed. She could now depart this spot leaving some old fears behind, while getting on with her life.

Upon leaving, she glimpsed the previously unnoticed, faded "For Sale" sign posted by the road. Thinking how precious to be able to come back here anytime, she'd definitely look into that possibility.

Beverly Waters McBride

 Chapter Eighteen

Maryville: Being Anish

All along, Beth wanted to enhance her knowledge of cultural crafts. She lucked into finding a few old souls left who agreed to teach their art. She learned about one elder from St. Ignace, about an hour south of Maryville, a renowned whittler and another, a weaver famous for her black ash baskets and cedar weaving who agreed to work with her. She found crafters who worked with old-time appliqué, inherited sewing patterns, beading, and leather and jewelry artists residing all around the countryside. Her friend, Ruth, knew all about the old pottery methods. Beth honored them all, becoming their motivated, enthusiastic student. She only had to ask with a tobacco gift and respect, then sit still long enough to listen. She usually heard some top-quality stories about the old days and life lessons thrown in, too. She grew especially close to Ruth, as they worked clay and then made the ancient underground pit to fire their work.

"Ruth, this is hard work," Beth croaked out, sweat pouring down her face as they prepared to fire some pots. "When I said I wanted to learn the old ways, I wasn't thinking about digging pits, placing work just so, covering it up and then digging it up again days later. Do you ever think of abandoning all this for that nice, clean, hard-to-work-with kiln for firing?"

Ruth chuckled. "Every time I do it," she responded. "Sure, that's okay for some, but it's not our way. Only a few are left who know the old way, or who want to learn. It's hard, all right. When things come out right, you can see for yourself that it's a thing of beauty. In our way, there's the element of the spiritual included as our secret ingredient. We pray over each phase, each piece, that it comes out right."

"I guess we'll be out here praying overnight again during firing this batch." She stretched her back and legs, thinking about their long vigil to come. The three of them, herself, Ruth, and Rose, Ruth's ten-year-old granddaughter, watched overnight. Rose managed to help sometimes. Mostly, she just liked to be in the outdoors overnight with her grandma. Beth expected Rose to form some great memories. She watched the granddaughter and grandmother huddled around a small fire under blankets listening to Ruth's stories. Ruth told old stories about animals and the moon and stars. Beth listened to Ruth's singsong voice telling ancient native stories about mythical creatures, the stars and the universe, Everyman and the Trickster, all favorite subjects of Native American lore and usually reserved for winter. She snuggled further into her warm blanket, allowing the stars above to fill her head.

She still had a lot to learn about Anishnabe culture, particularly about the role of women. Grateful for the extra time spent with Ruth, listening helped her feel proactive about addressing her information gap. She gained a glimpse of the "old ways," basking in the wisdom and honesty that flowed around Ruth. Her relationship with Ruth, the teacher, artist, grandmother, elder, woman and human being, unfolded like multi-sided box, with more than just lasting friendship, something like a kinship nestling in the center. She knew she'd learn more by being patient, despite feeling curious, so tamped down her urge to ask hasty and pest-like questions. Sitting under Ruth's wing, she listened while they worked. Ruth remained patient with her, although deemed herself free to loosen her sharp tongue if roused. Life lessons came gently with thought and humor, often disguised as mere conversation.

Today, they worked side-by-side making a soup in Ruth's cozy farmhouse kitchen. The room smelled of earthy scents of clorox and oil polish. Drying fresh herbs hung fragrantly above their heads from old rafters. They talked as she chopped fresh vegetables picked from Ruth's kitchen garden for their soup. The big stock pot, prized by Ruth for cooking her much loved recipes, released steam, reaching out like thin white tentacles of tantalizing aroma. The bubbling, liquid comfort was almost ready to taste. In Ruth's stick-built house, a few old barrels served as end tables, covered with long-ago crocheted doilies. Knickknacks perched on most every wobbly surface. The warped floor creaked when walked upon. Beth thought of it as the old house talking back, a sort of conversation, as you step down and it creaked back. An antique butter churn and flour mill from bygone days, still in regular use, reflected in bubble base glass oil lamps stationed around the room if needed, like soldiers on-call. While their supper simmered and the yeast bread rose undisturbed in the towel covered crockery bowl, they sat in aged but ever-so comfortable wooden rockers. The two of them quietly rocked, synchronizing their chairs like a ballet.

"Native women are the lifeblood of the community, never forget that," Ruth reminded Beth, almost out of the blue. Beth's brow furrowed, trying to discern the meaning of the message, expecting to glean new kernels of wisdom. "Women lead, too, and like men are important to the community as a whole. We can't speak for other cultures or tribes; we can only speak for ours, for Anishnabe," she said with finality. Ruth rocked gently, then said, "Each person eventually faces the Creator with their own tasks done or undone. That's the way it is."

Ruth stopped rocking, like punctuation in a poetic paragraph before resuming the steady, rhythmic rocking. They settled into a sort of cadence with each statement she stopped, delivering some profound insight, then commenced again, on to the next concept. Her eyes closed, as her usually busy hands rested on the rough fabric weaving in her lap. The chairs squeaked hypnotically on the ancient wooden floor planks. From her warm, peaceful cocoon, Ruth's voice soothed her senses. "Women are given the role of keepers of the water, like the fragile system of our northern lakes and rivers. In the summer months, a group of women walks around Lake Superior, trying to bring attention to preserving the lakes. We ought to be doing more to take care of the water flowing on Mother Earth."

"Women give life, but also keep the home and family," she continued, moving the ancient wooden chair again. "That's why we often give a blanket as a gift; it is a symbol of a warm and harmonious home."

After a while, Beth asked Ruth why some of the elder women gave stern looks to the young girls coming to the sacred fire or the pow-wow wearing their jeans or short skirts. "Women give respect to men and other women, and are respected in return. The same thing with the sacred fire. Women come to the sacred fire or spiritual events wearing dresses or skirts. It is out of respect for the role of women."

Beth listened to her, never before understanding the whole big deal about women being "required" to dress a certain way—now less like a requirement—it seemed more an honor. "When you explain it that way, I understand. It makes me feel good about being Anish and valued as a "quay," as a woman," Beth said.

Ruth nodded, pleased with her student. "Many women today don't understand their feminine role in the spiritual world, they chafe because of their lack of knowledge," she said. "Wearing a dress at important occasions, keeping the home together, raising your kids right or comforting the man in your life is liberating. It's all the better if he is one who follows the red road, has the same moral and ethical code as yours. A good man values his own role the same, neither higher nor lower than yours. Then you enjoy a partnership, a relationship blessed by Creator, in balance."

"Have you experienced that in your life, Ruth?"

Ruth stopped her rocking again. She looked straight ahead as if thinking about Beth's question, then gently rocked before she spoke. "Not completely, my dear. It took a lot of years for my old man to catch on, then he up and died." With a slight catch in her voice, she explained, "What can I say, except love won out in my youth. He was a handsome devil back then. We stuck together for a long time. You didn't meet my sweet Herb, did you?"

"No, he was already gone when I arrived on the scene. He sounds like a great person." Ruth sat quietly for a while, reminiscing to herself.

Then she spoke in low tones, "Speaking of how women should do," she added with a thoughtful pause, "too many times women end up with the urge to tear down other women by gossip or finding fault. That's a bad thing. More women should raise each other up, let go of negative gossip, and reign in those hateful words. That, to me, is also the measure of a woman: To recognize those she helped, what she's done to elevate others, the way she conduced herself in the community. Personally, I like to think there will be a fair accounting of me when the time comes," she said. Her voice became resigned, then hopeful.

"Ruth, you're gonna be bossing me around for a long time to come," Beth teased, using Ruth's own style of humor to boost her spirits. She nudged Ruth's arm.

Each time she opened up to really hear Ruth and Big Man, she grew spiritually. She looked forward now to going to the Women's Gathering in the spring, just as Big Man foretold.

Beverly Waters McBride

Chapter Nineteen

Sugar Island: Women's Gathering

Beth picked up Ruth, her car loaded with all their "camping" gear, for the ride over to Sugar Island on the ferry. It had been Big Man's idea that she do this. She had heard about the Women's gatherings, but had never been. Ruth, of course, knew all about it—said she went at every chance.

Waiting to board for the short trip over the river channel on the Sugar Island Ferry to the camp, a long line of trucks, cars, campers and vans lined up before and behind them. The unfamiliar rev and hum of the huge ferry engines, loud, and insistent, made her anxious. The other cars and trucks boarded the ferry with a lurching thud as tires hit the thin, narrow ramp to the ferry's broad, open deck. No one drove off into the frigid, dark water, but still a moment of uneasy tension lingered as their turn in the long line came. Flagged aboard, then directed to the middle of three rows of cars already idling on the deck, they packed in tight. Just when no room remained to accommodate any more, three more cars were directed aboard by the matter-of-fact deck hand. The hand then visited each vehicle to punch their passes or collect fees for the trip. They were actually sailing a mere five hundred yards or so across the shipping channel in the river. The short trip across the river channel itself conjured a much longer, more mysterious journey to a slower paced, less complicated version of rural town living. The horn sounded loudly, echoing up and down the channel, then the ferry launched, smoothly powered across to dock on the other side. All the vehicles then deboarded, to a repeat of the stomach clenching thud onto the pavement. Then, cars flew like bats out of hell over the smooth paved roads near the dock, rushing bumper to bumper up the steep, tree-lined hill centering the island. Several intersecting roads, unmarked and unpaved, trailed off to unknown destinations, one of which presumably lead to the Tribe's Culture Camp.

"Ruth, can you remember which of these unpaved roads goes to the camp?" Beth asked. "These directions aren't helping me so much right now. They must not believe in road signs out here in the woods." Annoyed, she chucked the map to the back seat in frustration.

"I'll know it when I see it," Ruth said, craning to see where they headed. "I guess we should be grateful the snow's melted, since the landmarks are harder to find covered in snow." She sat back, unconcerned. "You'll find it," she softly said, leaving Beth to reach back again searching for her paper map. "I like the winter gathering a lot," she offered. "It's cozy in the camp house. There are classes you know, in all kinds of new things. You can partake in whatever you want or even just sack out if you're too tired. You can be part of it or be apart from it. It's your choice. The cook does all the shopping, cooking those darn healthy meals they want for us elders, which is why I brought us a bag of chocolate for late tonight." She conspiratorially patted the huge bag of M&M's she smuggled in her canvas bag. "Sometimes we stay up late working on a project or singing or talking. We girls need our chocolate snacks. Hey," she said, pointing to a car in the distance in front of them, "just follow that car way up ahead of us, they're bound to be going to the same place."

Beth gunned the motor to catch up to them, just in case. Sure enough, following the car ahead, they lucked into finding the right road. The entrance sign to the camp posted at the gate looked pretty small to her. She might have missed it altogether. In the unpaved parking area cars parked every which way, while women busily unloaded cars, carrying luggage, trailing like ants into a building half-hidden by the trees up ahead of them. Beth drove slowly looking for a space to park, when a woman standing near the large double door to the main building spotted Ruth in the car. She directed them toward the loading zone at the front door to unload their bags. Beth kept the motor running as they unloaded, then pulled the car into an open spot she hoped was for parking.

Calling the building the "camp," Beth thought, didn't do it justice. Nestled in a clearing in an ancient forest of tall maples, oaks, aspens, and birches peppering the pristine setting, the main building looked deceptively small from the outside. Women wandered in and out, so it would require a pretty big space to accommodate them all.

To the right, several well-worn walking paths led to smaller structures that could still be seen through the quickly releafing trees. She'd like to walk around exploring the grounds sometime. She could see a big lodge with smoke coming out the top, and then a smaller sweat lodge in back. There was also a shed she surmised stored equipment for "sugar bush," the making of maple syrup in early spring. The surrounding land covered with hardwoods must be spectacular in the fall colors. Just now, the new growth sprouted everywhere. She spotted white trilliums close to the ground and dandelions about to spring into fluffy white fuzz balls, swaying in the cool gentle breeze. The tall trees grazed the roof of the main building.

Two women greeted them at the small porch overhang. Recognizing Ruth, they hugged her, asking if she needed help up the stairs to the sleeping dorms. "We want to honor our precious elders, you know,"

"Take either side," one said, motioning to the stairs inside, "It's only us girls here this weekend. Will you able to help Ruth fix up her sheets on the bunk? I can help if needed."

"Sure," Beth reassured, "I can take care of hers. I thank you for thinking of it."

Ruth went inside ahead through the door into a crowded and chaotic coat-hanging area, the floor surrounded on all sides with women's shoes, like a used shoe border. Coats hung on groaning racks, suitcases and plastic bags lay scattered everywhere in a big confusing jumble. "Brenda!" the woman shouted, "Ruth's here with her friend, Beth."

Beth cringed, embarrassed to draw attention, as they were soon surrounded by women all talking at once. Beth whispered to Ruth that she'd go up to the make the beds for them, so she slipped away to grab their gear and started up the wide, steep staircase to the dorm rooms above. Halfway up, someone grabbed a suitcase, saying "Let me help you with that." She looked around to see a short, sturdy, dark-haired woman in her early 30s reaching to help carry the load. She guided Beth to the top. They turned right into a huge open dorm area with at least fifteen beds, upper and lower, some with mattresses folded over. Some were already made up with colorful blankets or quilts on them. Tall windows, situated between each bunk with vertical blinds, held no curtains, so gave a view of the leafy green tops of the trees. Four low barrel chairs made haphazard seating on the far end of the room.

"Why don't you and Ruth choose these two, side-by-side, on the bottom?" She tossed the bags on the bed. "Hi, my name is Julie. You're Beth, right?" Julie extended her hand. Beth grasped it. Julie kept up a light chatter about the weekend and weather, as they made the beds together, laid out the pillows and towels for later. When they finished, they sat down on the beds a moment.

A muted sound of activity downstairs drifted up to them.

"Thank you so much, Julie. I appreciate your help. It's nice just to sit here for a little respite from all the confusion downstairs. You've been here before?"

"Yes. Please ask for help while you're here. Everyone here is very kind and wants to be of help. You're gonna have such a good time this weekend! I always do. I learn something new every time, not just the crafts or the lectures. It's fun to hang out with the other gals. I don't think it's just me. Most women stay focused on their own families. It's seldom that we take 'me' time, or let go and have fun. This is a safe environment. Some of the women I met here are now dear, dear friends.

Every time I see them in town, it just brings back all the fun. I love it."

"What are we in for, Julie?"

"Tonight after dinner, we'll partake of a big opening circle discussion. Brenda gives us an overview of the activities planned. What's really cool is that the time schedule is very flexible so we can keep going on with something that's fun. To me, it doesn't matter just exactly what we do, because I'm such a slave to the clock. Here, I try just to go along with whatever feels good to me. Things unfold as they are meant. That's it in a nutshell."

Julie launched into a narration of the amenities of the camp. "You'll find the bathrooms downstairs, including the showers. I'll let you wind down a bit, maybe rest a few moments. We'll be having dinner soon, you'll hear the dinner bell. We have a great cook and the coffee is on 24 hours in the kitchen! If you find yourself hungry, snacks will be out. You drink coffee?"

"Yes, mostly in the morning," Beth reported.

"If the coffee pot is empty, just start some up." Julie said as she rose to go back downstairs.

Beth sat down on the bed again. Her eyes closed for just a second to consider it all. Next thing she knew, she heard someone clanging a bell downstairs and fathomed this must mean dinnertime. She returned back downstairs on her slippered feet, following others descending to the call of the food, talking in excited tones, navigating the stairs. Tables and chairs had been set up in rows in the huge open room to accommodate the diners.

Ruth motioned her over and introduced Brenda, the brave and busy person in charge of the weekend. Brenda's smile lit up warmly upon meeting Beth. She gave them their camp packets, the manila envelopes containing agenda's, health surveys, resource sheets, and new pens for notes.

Brenda announced loudly to the group, "Let's all gather around for the blessing of the food, ladies!" All the women formed an elongated circle. The noise subsided as the women stood respectfully. The aroma of the cooking food reached them like a wave washing on a hungry shore. More women squeezed into the circle, shoulder-to-shoulder. Many of them brought their own colorful cloth dish bags, containing their plates and utensils for the meal.

"I gave tobacco to Ruth, one of our precious elders, to give us the blessing on our food. Thank you, Ruth."

Ruth stepped into the center of the circle, amidst the long tables. Some heads lowered, some heads turned in Ruth's direction, while others looked up or made eye contact with a friend within the circle. She held her tobacco offering in her hand as she sifted through it with her other hand, awaiting inspiration. She spoke in clear Ojibway language.

GZHEMINIDOO,

KIIN KINA GEGOO GAA-GIDNAMAN MAAMPII GIDKAMIG,

GDOO-MIIGWECHIWIN GII-HAAGDOWENMIIYAN GBEDBIG.

NAADMOOSHINAANG PANE BEKAADENDAMOWING,

MINO-AANGOONDWIN MIINWAA MINOWAAGOZWIN JE TEMGAG.....

..........MIIGWECH GZHEMINIDOO

When she finished, Beth and a few others thought her done with her prayer. But before they moved toward the food line, but Ruth began an interpretation of her prayer in English for the non-speakers. Everyone stayed in place to hear.

"I thanked the Creator for all the gifts we are given, for allowing this very special time together as women to renew, build our strengths, to rest, and to learn. We are the lifeblood of our families and our community. We have been given great responsibilities, but also great joys in doing our duties as mother, wife, daughter, sister and auntie. I prayed for blessings on the ones who prepared this food, provided it to us, so that its purpose may be manifested in the good words and deeds here and then shared back to our homes. I asked for blessings on those who wanted to be here but couldn't and to those who stayed behind to take care of things so we could come here. And for peace and harmony for all brotherhood. Amen. Annie, let's eat!" She grabbed the arm of one of her elder friends, and pulled her toward the front of the food line.

Brenda reminded the group that the elders go first in line. "Everyone use care going inside the kitchen to wash your dishes after dinner. Look out for the cook carrying heavy loads in there," she said.

Julie squeezed into line right behind Beth. "I enjoy someone else cooking, shopping and cleaning up. It's like being on a cruise!" she said.

They talked mostly about their hunger pains and how slowly the line moved. Julie loaned her an extra plate and fork from her own dish bag.

"We'll help you make a dish bag of your own this weekend. I always try to bring extras to events, since we try not to waste throwaway utensils, especially plastic and Styrofoam. It's easy enough just to rinse off dishes. Here we just wash them after we eat, then put them away in our dish bags ready for the next meal," she explained.

As those in the front of the line passed by on the way to be seated at the tables, parading their piled up plates before the now ravenous appetites down the line, they endured a gauntlet of hungry waiting women, impatient for their own turn at the food table. Tonight's menu was vegetable lasagna, fresh salad with buttered garlic bread, pudding and berry pie for dessert.

"The good part is it's all healthy, everything is made with low fat and low salt in order to accommodate any special diets," Julie said. "Between meals, they leave granola bars and fruit out so we may snack at our leisure. That's good for both the diabetics and the food addicts like me."

They balanced plates and drinks to sit at the end of one of the long tables, eating quietly for a while. Julie said to Beth, "See what I mean? Isn't this great. I try to cook healthier at home, too, but my boys are addicted to that fried stuff."

"Do you have a big family?" Beth asked her new friend.

"Just me, my husband and two boys, five and seven. They are a houseful. They keep me hoppin', for sure. One of my boys is in first grade at Tribal school. The baby goes to Tribal Head Start. He starts at Tribal school next year. How about you, you have kids?"

"No it's just me. Right now, I work as a night waitress at the casino lounge. I also draw and paint. Do you work, too?"

"Yes, I work part time for Intertribal Council doing clerical. I'll tell you all about it later." Beth hoped to learn more about her new friend as the weekend developed.

After eating, a big exodus to the kitchen occurred, to wash and stow away dishes, cleaning up.

Tables were removed and chairs formed into a massive circle for the next activity. The comfortable chairs filled up first, of course, latecomers found the fold-up chairs or floor pillows. Ruth sat in one of the plush living-room chairs, befitting her elder status, next to her friends. Julie and Beth made their way to two empty metal folding chairs.

Brenda made sure everyone was included in the one big circle. When everyone settled in, she warmly greeted the group. "Welcome, everyone, to the Spring Women's Gathering. It is a joy to see old friends and to meet new ones." She nodded as she met Beth's eyes. "We gather here as women of the tribe to celebrate, learn, and restore. We validate our commitment to family, sobriety, nature, community, family and the Anishnabe way of life. Each one of you belongs here. It is important that you accept responsibility for what you obtain from here to apply to your life. It's also up to you to determine what you wish to share about your growth with others." She paused, looking at the faces around the circle.

"If you look at the schedule for the weekend, we tweaked it to include a balance of rest, activity, lecture, participation, creativity, laughter and, of course, spirituality. No one's going to make you do anything for the next few days—your participation level is up to you. Sometimes, ladies come here to renew, finding that resting, sleeping, or just sitting, talking or even doing nothing is the very best for them. So we ask that you listen to your own inside voice or if you're praying, listen for the Creator to guide you. We want you to come away from here with whatever it may be you need to be filled, centered, and renewed."

She paused again briefly for all that to sink in. When everyone's eyes focused back on her, she said, "Tonight we are in for a special treat. Janice, our art therapist, is going to guide us through an expressive activity to kick off our weekend. Later on, any of you who want to go to the lodge next door to the fire, to pray or meditate may do so. Feel free to make your way over there at any point. Donna, you brought your fiddle?"

Heads strained to see her face, as the woman called Donna nodded, saying "Yep, we're gonna fire her up later on. I brought some song sheets this time, so get ready, gals!" Several applauded, several groaned. She'd never been much for singing by herself, but she might join in a group thing.

"Tomorrow, Dr. Lee is going to lead us in a discussion about some medical topics," Brenda continued. "She is always a great source of knowledge for us, so prepare your questions. The Health Service nutritionists are here again to help us with some nutrition activities about our diets. We expect to set up for several crafts projects, include making dish bags if anybody needs one. Tomorrow afternoon, we'll have a special presentation. We're all going to have foot and hand massages." A collective whoop went up!

"There are other things, too. You're going to eat well." Everyone applauded. Brenda motioned toward the kitchen as the cook peeked out. "Remember there's coffee and bottled water, along with juices, fruit and granola bars for the diabetics among us, so be sure to take care of yourself. Don't be shy about it."

"So, let's start by taking some deep breaths, getting in touch with the here and now. Let's settle in, relaxing in our chairs as we slow down our breathing. Let's close our eyes, become aware of our own breathing and the sounds around us in the room." Brenda loudly demonstrated taking in a big breath, holding it briefly, then making a big show of releasing it with a noisy exhale. "Now focus on the outside, the rustle of the trees, the breeze." She waited a few moments as the energy shifted and stress drifted away. After a little while, she said in the same soft, sing-song voice that lulled us all into a new relaxed frame of mind, "Now, everyone just come back in your thoughts to this room and raise one arm up over your head, as far as you can. Is everyone's hand up? Okay, now, let's all grunt like monkeys." She made grunting, monkey noises, scratching motions under her arms, and funny faces with pursed lips.

Eyes around the room popped open, as the laughter exploded. The room plunged into chaos. A few women, engrossed into the mirth of it, jumped up on their chairs, making monkey friends. The unexpectedness of the monkey noises was liberating. Women doubled over on their chairs, holding their stomachs in laughter. One woman ran to the bathroom, which set everyone to laughing again.

Ruth said to Brenda, over the din, "You've done it again, Brenda. How do you come up with this stuff? We'll never be the same after this."

Brenda said to the group, "It's all in fun. Remember there's a lot of healing in laughter. Let's go around the circle to introduce ourselves. Please give us your English name and for a twist this time, please if you wish, share your Ojibway name, how you obtained it, or what it means to you."

The women in the circle became reflective again. The introduction began to the left of Brenda, then to each woman in turn. Everyone listened respectfully, the custom in talking circles. After the intro circle, they drew pictures and discussed their artwork. Beth couldn't wait to participate in the art exercise. As an art therapist herself, she welcomed the chance to be just a participant for a change.

Afterwards, they stayed up singing and talking into the night, sharing stories about how they met their husbands and boyfriends, what transpired at their weddings. The stories spanned several decades. The sharing helped shorten the distance between them, as they grew to know each other. By time for bed, Beth felt strong connections as a member of the group. Her sense of belonging to the group added healing to her soul.

Loud snoring kept her tossing and turning until, exhausted, she fell asleep under her warm familiar blanket in this unfamiliar setting with its earthy sounds. She'd need a lot of coffee to make it through the day tomorrow.

Chapter Twenty

Sugar Island: Women's Gathering, Part Deux

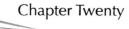

She woke up early, smelling the coffee brewing and the bacon cooking down below in the already warm kitchen. When she stumbled downstairs, the early risers were up already, helping set up for breakfast. She grabbed a warm mug of strong java and sat down at the table to ease into the morning. Some of the gals continued sleeping, foregoing breakfast altogether, in favor of a few extra moments of stolen rest.

Beth found her agenda, to go over the day's schedule. She wanted to take part in all the activities, so this promised to be a busy day. She noticed this morning's plan featured Dr. Vivian Lee, the Tribe's pediatrician.

Julie confided to Beth in a low tone before the circle started, "You know what I like about Dr. Lee?

She knows about kids, but she's good with the elders, too. Everyone wants her for as a personal physician. She gives you her best advice, but if you choose not to take it, she still cares about you, you know?"

Beth nodded. "I don't know her well, but it's pretty silly not to take her advice, since the doctor obviously knows what she's doing."

Dr. Lee both participated and presented at the Women's Gathering. Tall, and big boned, hair in a serviceable bun, dressed casually in a matching top and long skirt, she sat on the edge of her chair to see all the faces around the circle. She informed the group of women about issues specific to native health, then fielded general questions from the group. Participants expected to ask her burning questions about kids, medications, vitamins, or treatments, then answer with the unvarnished facts.

Dr. Lee had been a medical doctor for a long time, and lived in the community for many years. She had heard most everything at one time or another, no topic seemed out of bounds. She showed a great sense of humor, gesturing with her hand and unleashing her big booming laugh frequently.

After delivering a short "commercial" about heart disease in women, diabetes and high blood pressure, all keen topics in native health, Dr. Lee turned serious. "So, ladies, what do we know about menopause?"

Everyone sat still as if stunned. "I know, I know, I hear you saying, 'Doesn't everyone already know this stuff? Do people actually talk about this? Isn't this too personal?' You'll want to know these things, to care for your own health, as you mature. Armed with knowledge," Dr. Lee continued, "you make good choices as you spread good information with your sisters, even your own mother and aunties."

Beth listened in earnest, both fascinated and shocked about the workings of her own body, and what to expect to happen as she aged. Dr. Lee patiently debunked old myths and wives tales. She spoke frankly about life changes, raising consciousness about health with refreshing humor.

"...so bone density and retaining muscles become important, just as appropriate nutrition and portion size remain critical as you age," Dr. Lee said.

"It is good for us all to know these things," said Ruth, casually addressing the group. "In my day, we didn't talk about this even among the family, maybe because we didn't know." Many of the older women nodded. "It's good to speak of our health and for these young women and girls to know these things." As an elder, Ruth's opinion on the subject carried a lot of weight.

The group took a break after Dr. Lee's discussion.

Beth stretched, then walked over to thank Dr. Lee. "I appreciated hearing your information."

"Thank you, Beth," she acknowledged. "Remember, your experiences will be individual to you." Dr. Lee pointedly looked at Beth, then changed the subject, "You've been gone from here for a while, yes? Are you glad to be back? What have you been doing?"

Beth swallowed, unsure how to answer. It surprised her that Dr. Lee would take an interest in her. Although tempted to confide all she'd been through, her story loomed too large to tell now. Then, out of the blue, she choked on long held-back emotions.

Dr. Lee reached out to rest her hands gently beside Beth's head, saying low, "I see you've a lot going on inside, it shows all over your face, especially in your expressive eyes. Why don't you look me up later on, maybe we'll find some time this afternoon? That is, if you'd like to talk. I sense you may, eh?"

Beth only nodded. She'd love to talk to this smart, sensitive woman. She understood then how much she missed Charlotte, her warm friend, her saving grace during rough times in D.C. "That'd be great," Beth agreed, relieved. "May I find you some water or coffee or something now, Dr. Lee?"

"Thanks, no. I'll just stand in the ladies room line,

then go for a drink. I'll catch up with you later," she said, moving away, greeting people as she went.

Beth decided to walk outside for a breather, giving herself a chance to collect her thoughts. Stepping into the brisk spring air, she stood on the covered porch, taking in the slightly chilly fresh outdoor smell, then strolled over to the picnic table set up for the smokers, now empty. She sat enjoying the fresh rays of sunshine streaming down on her face through the newly green trees, as the wind fanned the grass and the white, low to the ground, early spring flowers. She sensed, rather than heard someone approaching, then sit down across from her, the wooden bench creaking with the new weight.

"Hello," said the young woman now sitting across from her. Beth's attention snapped back toward her new bench mate. "My name is Darlene. I don't believe we've met." They shook hands across the expanse of weathered wood table.

"Hello, Darlene, I'm Beth. Thank you for introducing yourself," Beth said.

"I wanted to speak to you after last night," Darlene said. "I loved our art therapy session. You must be an artist. I saw your drawing skills in your project and the way you explained it. I loved your color choices. We all got the same raw materials, you know, but yours came out like a piece of art. How'd you do that?"

"Thank you! Yes, I paint, sculpt a bit, and pot," she muttered, warming up to Darlene. "I'm hoping to land a job with the school system one day soon as an art teacher. I enjoyed last night, too. We all let out our feelings in color and form, then shared them with each other. Tell me what yours looked like?"

"Remember the all-yellow one with the blue background?"

"Yes, now I remember. I loved seeing your bold yellows. Do you make artistic things, too?"

"Well, yes and no. I work with the kids in Tribal Youth Ed. I'm the counselor who drives them all over in the van and makes them participate in activities good for them, like camps and tutoring. I also make sure they stay hydrated and fed when they're with me. We referee to keep them from whomping each other daily. Sometimes I make some creative crafts." Darlene shrugged. "We try to use many ways to engage them and keep their interest. It's hard sometimes."

"You must have a big heart and a lot of patience. It's hard to lead kids. People who work as youth leaders usually need the energy of three people. I'll bet the kids and their parents love you for it."

"Yes. I love what I do. It's pretty rewarding most of the time." Darlene hesitated. "Unfortunately, you can't please everyone, so what I hear most is what I haven't done. But I believe in the long run, I'm making a difference for the kids." She paused, thoughtfully, then said, "Say, could you come in sometime to organize an art exercise with them? Tell me what you'll need and I'll gather everything. I'll be your assistant, too. Super!" In her excitement, Darlene started talking fast, hardly taking a breath. Beth got caught up in her vibrant enthusiasm.

"Are you thinking about drawing, painting, crafts, ceramics, what?" asked Beth, her creative thinking now kicking in, too.

"Everything!" Darlene almost squealed in delight, clapping her hands enthusiastically. "Let's plan some projects. We can't pay you much. I'll try to arrange something for your time and for supplies. I'm so thrilled you'd even consider it!"

Beth understood why Darlene excelled at her job. "You sound so happy! Do you have a hard time finding folks to help you?"

"Sometimes. I wonder if people think that since we're getting paid, we ought to just see to it and not ask for help." She paused, as if saying something she shouldn't. "Then, other volunteers are totally selfless, devoting their time and talents to the kids in great ways. You're going to be one of those, I am sure. When our helpers jump in, it keeps the program fresh, frees us up to address the many other needs not being dealt with at home or school. Every now and then, they enjoy seeing a different face. I mean, we're limited in what we tackle."

Beth agreed to visit Darlene's office during the next week to make some plans. Together, they walked back inside for the next group activity on the agenda.

The instructor for the activity spread the center table in the room with colorful crafts materials, sequins, beads of all kinds, ribbons, and yarns.

"We are making a yarn, string, and bead concoction to depict the passage of time in one's life or path, or in remembrance of people or life events. It's called a 'Time Ball'," the instructor said. Some participants dove in, grabbing supplies for making their balls, some held back as if waiting for inspiration. Beth pondered how to organize her lifeline, then she worked quickly, focused on creating her time ball.

She kept working even as the exercise evolved into the next phase. The women again sat in the circle, listening as each described treasured personal moments caught on their "time balls." She squirmed as the turn to speak moved closer, thinking about running away to the bathroom, but her new friend Julie supportively touched her arm, instinctively knowing somehow anxiety built inside.

When her turn arrived, Beth held up an intricate macramé weaving, the work of an artist, no doubt.

"Mine is in remembrance of some of the people who helped me," she explained. "I tried to remember each one, then I added this one white bead on to represent both the ones I forgot and the ones who helped me that I didn't know about. The three strands represent mind, body, spirit. They are separate at times, then woven together in better harmony toward the bottom. It is unfinished, and since it's unfinished for a while yet, much more is yet to add. I chose to honor people, good people, rather than events, because I found there's good helpers, even in the worst of times." She laid her heart out with her words for all to see.

Afterward, the other women gathered around her, telling her what a lovely work of art she produced.

"I love your ideas," one said.

"The colors you chose are very inviting," said another. She thanked them modestly.

When they all met back together, Brenda summed up the time ball experience. "Every person has represented their own feelings and experiences in a way comfortable to themselves. Many shared their emotions, allowed others to move closer. That's the beauty of our weekend, to reclaim a special connection with each other, let go of the isolation that separates us, keeps us at a distance from each other in the modern world. Here and now, we have permission to be vulnerable, to share it, and then be stronger for it. This exercise caused you to stretch, to be creative, and you did it. It's been beautiful."

Later they heard a presentation about the benefits of massage. Beth's name wasn't drawn for the full massage, so she participated with the others in the foot massaging lesson, both giving and receiving.

"Don't you dare tickle my feet," warned Julie.

"Hey, I'm just following directions," Beth quipped.

"You know, before today, I was a little leery of anyone touching my feet," Julie confided. "That's just me. I'll admit, though, this feels great. You could do this every day for me," she joked.

"You bet," said Beth, "although following you around might get old, Julie. You'd better teach your husband the skills."

"Now that's funny," said Julie. "Like that's gonna happen."

After a sumptuous lunch of Indian tacos, the afternoon schedule called for free time. Women napped, walked outside, read long-neglected novels, or chatted. Others worked on crafts.

Looking around the big room, Beth noticed the bulk of chairs arranged in small groupings, personal belongings left behind, a book spread open upside down, a forgotten shawl draping the couch, and pillows in disarray. The space felt comfortable, without stress. Low conversations gave way periodically to subdued laughter.

"I love that everyone feels included in this weekend," Julie said in her characteristically low, calming voice. "You just play it out as you wish. It's seldom I choose an activity or just to go nap if I want. It's great just to stop. I almost don't know what to do with myself."

"I agree," said Beth. They conversed a while, then Beth said, "I think I'll go upstairs to rest a little while."

Julie waved her up the stairs with a warm, "See you at dinner."

Beth lay down on her bunk, relaxing. She drifted off, awaking a short while later, having taken what served as a "power nap." She looked around slowly, reorienting to the room, then spotted Dr. Lee, sitting alone in a comfy chair down the long room, near the far windows. Beth watched her for a moment as she read a book, raised her head to look thoughtfully out the windows, before tearing her attention back to the book open on her lap. Beth wondered if that meant Dr. Lee might well rather be outdoors, yet believed in using her free time reading her book.

After a while, Beth roused, stretched and then walked quietly near Dr. Lee's chair, waiting for acknowledgement.

"Hi Beth, feel free to join me," she offered, marking her spot in the book as Beth slipped into the chair across from her. "Thanks for saving me from this very dull article. I try to keep up on the journals."

"I hope I'm not disturbing you, Dr. Lee."

"Please call me Viv. No, not at all. I'd like to hear more about your art. We've seen each other around town, but never took a chance to talk," Viv said in a comfortable way.

"You've been here a good long time, eh, Dr. Lee, uh, Viv?" Beth asked, remembering to use her first name.

"Yes, fifteen years. I'm almost a fixture here now. When I came here from Tennessee, I held no idea this would become my home. That's just the way it turned out. I liked the people here and they liked me. Time passed quickly. I brought my mother here a few months back to live with me now. It's great to have her here with us."

"Wow, that's quite a change, humid south to deep cold," agreed Beth.

"That first year I found living here a difficult adjustment. Over the years, I guess I grew to like it, too. Now I enjoy teasing the newcomers to this part of the country. They have no idea what they're in for, with the snows and winter temps. I get a big kick out of hearing their big talk at first, then asking them midwinter if they felt the same.

Up the Creek

You grew up here, right, Beth?"

"Yes, I came here in elementary school from downstate. My father came from here, then the family moved to Detroit. I was born there. Many Tribal folks relocated down there, trying to make it in the city. I'm told that my family was sidetracked into drugs, alcohol and legal issues. I came here as a young girl to stay with my elderly aunt, Aunt El. She tried her best with me, of course. We both found it an awkward fit at first. As I grew, we became closer. I cared for her until she died several years ago. The rest of my family never kept in touch, so I don't know much about them." Beth sighed, wondering how she managed to rattle on so far into that subject. She didn't know why, but it kept on coming out.

"Recently I received a call from downstate about my long-absent mother. I haven't heard from any of them in Detroit for years. Now my mother is sick and wants to connect with me, so my aunt called to feel me out. A part of me wants to tell them it's too late now. It's not up to me to make them feel less guilty at this point in time." Viv's brow furrowed as she grasped the explanation, then waited for the next revelation.

"Another part of me wants to just rush in, hoping for family that really wants me, like a little kid, hoping for something. I couldn't stand to be pushed away for some reason by these people again."

Viv listened quietly. "I hear the anxiety in your voice," she said. "How are you going to handle it?"

"I'm not positive yet. I'm just sure I don't want to churn it over in my mind, or relive old hurts, or be so needy."

"I expect that you'll contact your mother, despite all your hesitation," Viv responded. "You're strong enough now to deal with whatever comes of it. What do you think?"

Beth just blinked at her. "You know, I think I'll try it. I couldn't be so strong to deal with it before coming here. Thank you for hearing me out, Dr., uh, Viv."

"I see you feel much better about this decision. What can I do to help you with it?" she asked with gracious sincerity in her voice.

"May I check in with you, after? I may need to talk it over."

"Of course, please keep me in the loop."

They looked at each other for a moment, then Beth blurted out, "I admire your dedication and expertise at work for the people of The Tribe. I appreciate what you taught us this morning. I had no idea how little I knew about the workings of my own body or what to expect in the future. That's a real service you do."

"I hear that sentiment each time we hold of these

circles. The Women's Gatherings are great for being able to reach the very women who benefit most from the information. Women are curious and receptive to the truth, as you heard this morning, about everything from flu vaccines to arthritis. I think people are sharing their new knowledge with their friends, sisters and neighbors, too, becoming aware."

The two women lapsed into companionable silence.

"I seem to remember that you used to play the ladies hand drum and dance at pow-wow. Do you still do that, Viv?" inquired Beth.

"Yes, it's a commitment, you know. I think our drum group will be here tonight out in the lodge, if you'd like to come."

Beth nodded. "I think I'd like that," she said thinking it might be nice to be part of a group like that.

"Beth, you seem to have more stories to tell. It sounds as if you've already overcome a lot of negative experiences. The look in your eye draws my curiosity, makes me believe you are shouldering a huge burden all by yourself and could use some support or at least a listening ear. Does that ring true with you?"

Beth looked at her. Viv's sincerity struck her as completely trustworthy. Her eyes held concern, nothing more. Beth's anxiety and doubts welled up, as a giant tear rolled involuntarily down Beth's cheek.

"Oh my goodness," comforted Viv, as she grasped Beth's hand in both of hers, patting the back of Beth's hand, 'oohing' and 'ahhing' in sympathy, just waiting, in case Beth wanted to say more.

"I've been going through a lot. Most of the time, I handle it. Sometimes the old despair creeps up and then I return to rational thinking again."

"I understand," Viv acknowledged, just listening.

"As a kid, I saw a hodgepodge of colors and shapes," Beth drew her hand back and forth across her forehead, "so I thought everyone saw the same things. Much later, I learned that actually I see things differently than other people—I perceive color and combinations differently. I think of it as a gift for unique perspectives of ordinary objects. It's sometimes been a burden, but at other times my saving grace. I tried to tamp it down for years, trying to fit in, to be like everyone else. In recent years, I've learned to allow the expression of my artistic voice. I am able to help others, especially the children, to find their own creativity. Does that make sense?"

Viv nodded, letting Beth tell her story in her own way.

"I'm refuse to be a victim anymore. Early events of my life cast me in the role of the victim of uncaring or incapable parents, then to unsatisfying personal relationships and ultimately, abuse." Beth decided to leave that topic there for now. "I am choosing to let those go now, to take responsibility for my own happiness, comfort and success from now on. Lately, I connected with some good counseling and therapy, but the victim mentality is quite pervasive. I still have some recovering to accomplish." She wiped her eyes with a tissue out of a box in the middle of the table in front of her. Someone thoughtful anticipated needing a box of tissues on this table this weekend.

She breathed in, then launched in a different conversational direction. "I worked in DC at a gallery of African Art before coming back here. I managed to obtain my BA and MFA. I made some wonderful friends there, but I felt a pull to return to my 'ground,' so here I am. Big Man convinced me recently that my emotional safety net is derived from strength inside, not a location, so I'm coming to grips with that notion." She blew her nose, in a non-lady-like honk that made them both giggle.

"I have a little art studio down by the river now. I work night shift at the Casino lounge to keep me out of trouble. That's my story. A lot of good is going for me, too. I'm hoping for an art teaching job here in the school system. I just spoke to Darlene about doing some projects with the Tribal Youth Program. Do you know Darlene?"

Viv nodded. "It's impressive that you sound so upbeat and confident about your art. Those kids sure need your skills. They thrive on adult attention. I bet I see most of them regularly, too. A few of those kids, even families, desperately need your skills. If I can help you, please let me know." Beth believed Dr. Lee might even deign to dirty her hands with paints and clay, if it would help the children.

They talked of less consequential things for a while. When the dinner bell rang, they remained loathe to move from their intimate cocoon, until Viv's stomach rumbled loudly. They jumped up together, making their way downstairs to join other women in the noisy bedlam of the pre-dinner line.

They finished out the weekend, enjoying the food and companionship. On Sunday, the women rushed to pack, load and catch the ferry on every half hour for scheduled departures for the mainland. Clean-up time arrived for the handful remaining to scrub down the building grounds and kitchen.

Brenda said, "The camp admin always love the ladies gathering, since we clean the rooms so thoroughly before we go, It doesn't see that kind of cleaning until we come back next time." They single-mindedly progressed with their vacuuming, scrubbing and straightening.

Sentimentally, Beth hated to leave the camp. "I sure enjoyed being here," she told Brenda. It amazed her that just four short days ago, the camp and most of the people were virtually unknown to her, but now she couldn't imagine not having her new friends, just as Big Man had foretold.

They waited in the line for the return ferry to break the connection to the gathering on the island for this trip. Ruth sighed, dozing beside her in the passenger seat, as they waited. She saw the Canadian geese soar around them, then landing in the frigid water beside the dock. Like her thawing heart, the water in the lake warmed as each day passed.

Beverly Waters McBride

# Chapter Twenty-One
Maryville: Dojo

Beth sat inside her car parked outside the well-lit Martial Arts studio, to watch for a while. The big glass windows of the brightly lit dojo brought cheer to the otherwise dark strip of stores on the busy main drag, if you call a rural town after dark busy. She saw the activities inside, yet they couldn't see her observing. By learning some protective skills she might perhaps take care of herself should the need arise. The exercise couldn't hurt either. Still she hesitated, since the thought of actually starting classes overwhelmed her.

At first, she saw young kids scampering through the open door into the classroom wearing their adorable white suits in childlike disarray. They sat on the floor, removed shoes and socks, bowing as they entered the practice area to start stretching. In a few minutes, a few adults ambled through the door. She knew some of the other students already. They attended by skill level, rather than age or gender. Screwing up her courage—soon—

very soon, she wanted to give it a sincere try. Cost wasn't holding her back either. Perhaps sending some work for exhibit, or at least consignment, would be an incentive to push her forward to sign up for the Karate class. At least paying for it by selling a few items might remove one more false barrier to signing up.

In her heart, she believed taking a tangible step toward becoming self-sufficient, self-preserving, and self-protecting to be huge for her personal healing process. Time for her to jump the fence, or jump into the one canoe as the saying goes, over to health and wellness.

She jumped a little in her seat, when a knock on her car window surprised her. She recognized Betty, an old high school friend, standing outside her car, waving at her. She rolled down the window.

"Betty! Good to see you. What are you doing here?" she asked with an edge of hopefulness in her voice.

"Hey, Beth, long time, no see! Are you coming in for class?"

"No, not yet. I'm building up my courage by watching from out here tonight. Are you in it?"

Betty shook her head, "Not my cup of tea. My kids work on their belts so I bring them twice a week. You ought to go ahead, jump in! Lots of women go into it now, it's a good thing. It's done wonders for my boys. They developed good discipline and concentration. It helps their grades somehow, too. Even their manners improved. I'm all for it. You should do it, Beth!"

Beth mumbled low, "Soon, that sounds good," as Betty, distracted said, "Oops, gotta run. Hope you make it inside soon." She disappeared inside a sea of white suited, pre-class excitement.

Still reluctant to leave her car, Beth watched as the class started. After watching a while, she backed her car out of the space, continuing the drive to work.

She preferred going to the lounge early, anyway. She liked chatting and laughing with her friend, Marty, the bartender. He heard her expound often about her dreams for teaching. A great listener in the vein of all bartenders, he listened to her talk about her desire to teach.

"Marty, I can't wait to set up my own classroom," she said often. "I'd love nothing more than to release the artist lurking inside some unsuspecting childlike psyche. My whole lifestyle would be different—my time and schedule, too—more normal, like the rest of the world."

"Do you hear yourself already calling them your kids?" Marty reminded her that she thought way too far ahead.

"Yes, I hear it. I know. I haven't even started yet and I already love it."

For now, she'd be content to waitress during the risky early evening hours and to sleep, paint, and think during the more productive daytime hours. Determined not to be a flaky artist, she actually looked forward to imparting some appreciation, if nothing else, in the hearts of beautiful, open, busy children. She knew firsthand that creativity might be just under the surface, out of sight, waiting to be discovered, or as in her case, unleashed.

Here she stood, wearing the all-white, stiff, brand new gee, about to launch into something new. "This thing is not real comfortable," she mumbled to herself, "and it gaps." Clutching the neckline of her gee, wishing she had a safety pin. Already perspiring before any exertion, hoping she remembered as well as those young kids beside her, she remained open, hopeful that her grownup body survived this new training, this new chapter in her rise from victimhood.

Finally, other women about her age arrived. "Are you able to do okay on the exercises?" she asked them. One said, "Sure, maybe slow at first, but I stuck with it."

"I hoped for a suit without the gap in the front," Beth said self-consciously, slapping her chest.

"Don't worry, you're wearing a t-shirt underneath, nothing usually gets exposed. You rearrange your shirt when you need to."

She followed Master Green, while watching him in the huge wall mirror, mimicking his movements. After class, Master Greene came over to her to speak to her.

"Wow, Miss Morrison, you moved very well for a beginner." His warm smile charmed her as he sought out her eyes. "You've done this before? You're very determined."

"No, sir," she replied. "I did the usual aerobics and some skiing. For a while I played on a women's hockey team in the Canada league."

"Women's hockey, eh?" he said, as if that explained a lot. "I see a lot of strength in your movements tonight. I hope you'll keep it going. Your focus is very good. You'll get the hang of it quickly. If you come a little early next time, I'll go over the form with you individually or one of the other students can show you. Even the kids enjoy helping. We train everyone that way, to assist." His eyes twinkled when he spoke. Muscular, medium height, with wide shoulders, narrow hips and equal facial features, he'd likely not be described as handsome, but he wasn't unfortunate-looking either. He conveyed the prospect that you'd not want to face control unleashed in a fight, gentle, yet not unintimidating. His dark gray eyes danced when he laughed, then showed another intensity altogether as he taught his students. She liked it.

They bowed to each other as she left the mats, since that showed respect to the teacher.

She spoke to another student on the way out, "That workout was intense. I'm out of breath."

"Well, just keep with it. I'll help you," her classmate promised. "Oh, you'll most likely feel every muscle tomorrow after all that new movement. Just take warm shower tonight and relax tomorrow. It's fun, though, eh?"

Beth stood watching the next class of advanced students leaping and kicking into the air. She expected to leave the leaping to the young ones. She thought the movements beautiful though, like choreography.

She went back for class number two later that week. This time the routine looked a little more familiar. People in the class greeted her in welcome.

"You're doing great, Beth," Master Greene told her after class. He sought her out after each session to speak to her, to encourage her. "If you keep up the pace, you'll be in the next belt, pronto. I'd like to see you try for it, maybe in the next few months, eh? We're having an exhibition at a fitness festival next month in Canada. Please come with the group, to run through a mini class showing folks what we do. With the group," he added again quickly, when her head shot up abruptly.

"Sure, if you think I'll be ready," she told him.

She appreciated that he seemed to like her, but kept the necessary professional distance, as her teacher should.

She loved the workouts. The discipline of the martial arts felt good to her. "It's like a test of yourself every time," she confided in Marty one night before work. "I thrive on the discipline. I'm practicing at home, going to the dojo at every chance. The other students help me learn as well. That's how I've been able to achieve some pretty rapid advancements, even if I say so myself," she said with pride.

Marty didn't need a crystal ball to see it suited her. "With this, as with most everything else you try, when you apply yourself, you excel. I'd hate to run into you in a dark alley, 'cause your mad skills don't show on your sweet face, you know," he observed. Beth loved him for encouraging her growth in his silent supportive way.

One day, after an exhibition at a children's festival, Master Green mentioned that maybe sometime they could go for tea. She raised her eyebrow, "I thought you didn't do tea," she teased, "something about your body being a temple." What a fine temple it is, too.

"Yes, that's true, I try to keep a simple diet and schedule. It wasn't really the tea I wanted, but to spend some non-work time with you. You know that, smarty." They grinned at one another. She decided to give him a YES to going for that herbal tea after class.

That evening, she parked her car facing the building in front of the dojo, reaching to the seat beside her to grab her gear. Her eyes glanced inside the building. She froze. It couldn't be. She looked again. There, working out in the dojo, her dojo, stood Dan Walkin. While she knew he held black belts, she hadn't run into him there before, so he didn't know about her developing skills.

She couldn't go in with him there, big as life. It was just too much, too embarrassing to have him there watching and judging her. She held no animosity toward him, so it shouldn't matter, but she'd cross that bridge another tonight.

She restarted her car, pulling out of the lot. If she wanted tea, she'd go by herself tonight. She admitted to being a coward. She'd deal with that tomorrow, just like Scarlet O'Hara. Fiddle-de-dee.

Next day, time on her hands, Beth opted for her favorite lunch at Penny's Kitchen. She loved the turkey Rubin subs there, piled high with sauerkraut, a dill wedge, and accompanied by fragrant Kenyan coffee. Yum! They knew her at the deli counter and that she always took a long time reading the whole menu posted high above the counter, but almost always ordered the same sandwich. After placing her order, she found an empty table to watch people and enjoy the surroundings. She liked the little flower vases on each table, looking at the artwork for sale and posters hanging on the brick walls in the converted warehouse. She'd try to remember to ask about hanging one of her pieces there.

When her order arrived, it looked like a tall sandwich tower rising above the white restaurant plate, surrounded with a mote of crisp, crinkle potato chips. She quickly moved the pungent, wet, dill wedge to a napkin to keep from sogging up the chips. Nobody likes soggy chips.

She dove in, taking a big first bite, savoring the taste of the smoked turkey, melted Swiss cheese, dressing, and sauerkraut juices, as it dripped down her face, along her arms, practically all the way to her elbows. She used up many napkins on this beauty. Between bites, her eyes closed in appreciation.

Slowly it registered that someone stared at her. She swabbed her chin with her napkin, chuckling, fully expecting to see someone pointing toward her as she enjoyed this exquisite, albeit juicy sandwich. A fleeting shadow passed by outside, out of direct view at the edge of the big front window. She squinted to see who might be there, unable to make them out. Looking around again, she found no one there. Oh, well. These babies are messy. Sorry, and bite me!

She remembered a few other odd times lately having an eerie feeling of being watched. Awareness shifted in her head, back over the last few days. She shrugged again, then went back to enjoying the wettest lunch ever.

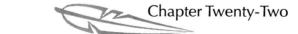

Chapter Twenty-Two

Luvenia's Secret Wedding

Everyone in town already knew all about the "secret" wedding of Luvenia Phelps to Paulie Denver. Their not-very-clandestine relationship enraged her father, Sheriff Phelps. Everyone knew, too, that Luvenia, now pregnant, intended to marry Paulie. Their big secret wedding happened to be not so secret after all. Poor Sheriff Phelps, she thought, still believes he controls his house. He must be in shock to discover that shy, little Luvenia now has her own opinion, especially concerning Paulie. Clearly, everyone but her father saw that they loved each other. They defied all naysayers to be together, whatever the cost.

As a teen, Beth frequently babysat for the Phelps girls. She wanted to be at the wedding, despite the Sheriff's profound disapproval. If only on the edge of the Phelps family dynamics, she had watched the girls growing up. She was still a little intimidated by big, muscular, loud Sheriff Phelps; however, petite Mrs. Phelps, on occasion, stood toe-to-toe with him, despite her diminutive stature. Beyond holding her own, she almost always prevailed. Even though he blustered, controlling and impatient, he usually "came around" to please his wife.

The reception would take place at the Tribal Cultural Center. At these community celebrations, Big Man always led the Native Ceremonials. Father Bob, from the Ojibway Catholic Mission, performed the church version. Their friends in the Tribal community expected to pitch in and help for the celebration. People enjoyed giving to the new couple, even if the gift proved more a token offering. Beth appreciated yet again the kind, generous nature of native people, even when controversial, like now, since no one wanted to offend the Sheriff.

Beth stopped at the Phelps' house one afternoon to ask Lovie's mother how she could help. They sat down at the kitchen table while Mrs. Phelps described arrangements so far for the big day.

"You know about Big Man and Father Bob," she said smiling. "The ceremony itself will go on in the pow-wow arena. Paulie's friends will make the cedar canopy and all the outdoor arrangements. Big Man usually takes care of the sweat lodge ahead of time. Some of my friends are taking over cooking the food for the dinner after the ceremony. The menu keeps expanding, so I know there'll be plenty to eat." She beamed with gratitude for all the help. "I'm not sure what you might bring," she looked around, flustered, then lit on a solution. "Could you maybe bring a dessert or something like that, Beth?"

"Are they going to have a wedding cake?" Beth asked, "Because if you'll allow me, I'd love to supply a little wedding cake."

"Sure, if you want to. That'd be great! Now, no one expects you to overdo it. We all appreciate your offer very much, Beth. Just coming to be with us is gift enough, you know."

"I'll certainly come across with more than just that. Please, let me just take over that whole cake part, decorate the table, and the serving plates, napkins, you know, all that stuff?" While she would have agreed to finance the whole wedding, she understood the importance of sharing responsibility both duties and pleasures in the community.

She contented herself to furnish a layered wedding cake with all the trimmings. Of course, she planned to go way overboard expressing her own style. She had carte blanche. Mrs. Phelps hugged her again right there at the table, in thanks, before turning serious a moment later.

"I guess you heard my husband, the big, strong Sheriff, is against the wedding. He won't take any part of it?"

"Yes, I heard. I can't believe he means to stubbornly hurt anyone," Beth nodded sympathetically. "You believe he'll eventually come around, yes?" she asked, more hope than certainty in her voice.

"I'd like to think so, but he's really upset. It's going to kill Lovie not to be given away by her father. Her heart's been set on it since she was a tiny girl." Tears welled up in Mrs. Phelps kindly, dark eyes. Beth wished she knew how to turn this around for all of them.

As she grew up, Mrs. Phelps stood as a great role model in her very vulnerable teen years. She had been a teenager without a mother, with only an elderly aunt in the picture. Mrs. Phelps listened as Beth shyly talked about her teenage issues. She never passed judgment and hardly ever lectured. She may have gently given a caution or suggestion, if called upon. On top of much-needed support, they'd paid her for babysitting the sweet little girls to boot. They never discussed it, but Mrs. Phelps and the girls meant a lot to her.

Later that week, Beth kicked into wedding-cake frenzy. She scoured the best bakery in town—actually the only bakery—ordering a multi-tiered cake extravaganza, with an elegant caketop, matching napkins, plates, and cake servers, monogrammed bride and groom champagne flutes and real flowers. She also made arrangements to set up the cake table at the cultural building. She wanted to make it elegant, in a down-home, casual sort of way. She wanted people to be comfortable with the spread, not to "put on the dog," as she once heard pretentiousness described. She fought back the urge to commission an ice sculpture, since that might be construed as going a little too much over the top.

The day of the wedding, Beth left home early to pick up the cake in order to set it up at the Cultural Building. A sealed bottle of fine champagne for the happy couple sat in a nearby basket. While she doubted the paper doilies were utilized much at local community events, she refused to compromise. She stood back to admire her finished handiwork. It looked as gorgeous as she had hoped, simple and tasteful. She couldn't wait to see the look on Lovie's face when she saw her elegant cake.

Lovie arrived at the building early, too. She came over to see the cake table, thanking her profusely.

"It's so beautiful, Beth, just like a real wedding cake," she said, tearing up already, overwhelmed with all the arrangements for the big day, just as any blushing bride.

"It is a real wedding cake, Lovie, your real wedding. I remember us talking, you must have been all of nine years old. You wanted a big white wedding, a princess dress and nothing short of Prince Charming."

"Paulie's not exactly the Prince Charming–type," Lovie said, stars practically shining from her eyes. "But I love the heck out of him and he makes me happy. We laugh, we even cry. He takes care of me, Beth. That's what I really want. Right now, I'm happy one minute, then sad the next that my dad won't be here. He's just unreasonable." She dismissed it all with a swipe at the tear in her eye and a wave of her hand. "You know all about it." Her frustration surfaced as her big, tear-filled doe eyes turned sad.

"Lovie, I wish you the very best," Beth patted her soothingly on the back. "You're a grown woman now, your baby is coming. That rascal, Paulie, hangs on your every word, like you hung the moon. Your daddy loves you. He'll come around when you show him how you're happy, that you're still going to get your education and raise your family right. Your job today is to be a beautiful, blushing bride, without having teary-eyes or a red nose for your wedding photos."

"You're going to take pictures, too? Beth, you're the best." She hesitated, looking down apologetically, quiet for a moment. "Sorry I stole that lipstick out of your purse back in the old days." Beth eventually comprehended her childlike confession.

"You took it? Wow, yes, I looked everywhere for that lipstick. I thought I lost it. You had to be just ten years old. Do you remember that far?"

"Yes, I still have it. I was scared to throw it out all these years—ashamed, too. It's all dried up, but still haunts me, hidden in my little, private cigar box. I love you Beth, for all you've done, for this beautiful wedding cake and all." She started crying again, hugging Beth, who cradled her youthful face in both hands, wiping Lovie's tears away with her thumbs.

"You run on, enjoy your day." Beth, blinking back her own tears, gently lowered her hands onto Lovie's shoulders, and turned her toward the area closed off for the bridal party with a playful push on her back. Lovie waved, then skipped over to bevy of excited bridesmaids. Beth watched her skip off, still a young girl at heart, about to take on adult responsibilities. If good wishes possessed healing powers, in that moment Beth directed all toward Lovie, the blushing bride, and Paulie, her Prince-Charming-by-default.

Beth wandered to the pow-wow grounds to look at the cedar canopy and take a few pre-wedding photos of the arena. As the unofficial photographer, she'd prepared several cameras with a variety of lenses, ready to capture any special moments that came her way. She used digital cameras so there'd be no rolls of film to develop later. She planned to produce a photo scrapbook for Lovie and Paulie as a gift. She also hoped to make one for Lovie's mother.

A large crowd already milled around outside the cultural building. Gifts weighed down the gift table, overflowing onto the blankets spread on the surrounding floor. Photo ops hit her at every turn. She kept reminding herself to stick to taking record shots, rather than art shots, or she'd fill up her memory card on just the interesting wood pile stacked up near the Cultural Center fireplace.

She focused instead on the groups of people talking. When she saw Dr. Lee, they started walking toward each other until Dr. Lee was halted by one of her talkative patients. Melinda waved at her, pointing out her whole brood, children running amuck as usual. She found her new friend, Julie, after they almost literally ran into each other. Nothing spilled, thank goodness. Julie excused herself to go to the kitchen to help.

She spotted Dan, serving today as Paulie's best man. Their eyes connected, and he winked at her, before he went to take care of best man business. She snapped a few touching shots of him calming the groom with his hand on Paulie's shoulder, straightening his ribbon shirt in a very big brotherly fashion. Someone wove together a circle of daisies for the bride and groom to wear like crowns, yet Paulie self-consciously held off putting it on until the last minute.

Evidenced by the huge crowd, Lovie's father's objections only added interest in the event. Despite the cloud hanging over it, people wanted to be there. Laughter and muted conversation rose and fell from the crowd.

Beth snapped photos of Lovie and her sisters and mother getting her ready. She wore the traditional white leather, fringed, beaded wedding dress. It fit like a glove on Lovie's still slim body, only a slight telltale tummy bulge to show for the upcoming newest family member. Her hair hung long, straight down her back. The wreath of white daisies rested full and natural on her dark, shiny hair.

When a commotion sounded near the front door, Luvenia's sisters peered out from the partition, froze, then almost shrieked, "It's Daddy! He's here!" They all rushed to the partition opening, stood transfixed, one head above the other, in awe at seeing the reluctant, imposing Sheriff Phelps near the doorway of the building, hat in hand, flanked by Dan and Harry, Melinda's husband.

No one present denied the importance of his actually appearing for the wedding. He fit right in, since everyone there knew him as neighbor, friend or relative. Most had voted for him repeatedly over the years.

Lovie ran out into the crowd to see for herself, then ran up to her father, hung on his neck, kissing his face, as tears streamed down both their cheeks.

"Daddy, I'm so glad you're here. Thank you, thank you, it means so much to us," she blubbered out with all her emotions sounding in her wavering voice. He staggered back a bit from the force of her jump. He wrapped her up in his strong arms.

Beth backed away to allow them their privacy, as the whole family circled him, hugging him and each other.

She walked outside, snapping shots of the people assembling on the pow-wow grounds. She stood close to the front near the cedar canopy to document the ceremony itself, at least the parts permissible to photograph. She knew not to snap indiscriminately any of the ancient sacred moments. Big Man would no doubt remind them also when the time came.

A rare UP warm, sunshiny, breezy day was a good sign. She pondered how a day was cool and warm at the same time. When a pair of butterflies drifted in, circling the couple, she couldn't resist some close ups of nature's playmates, following them with her camera as they tumbled lazily around the couple. Sighs of awe rippled through the guests, recognizing the significance of such a visitation from nature.

Grandmothers and Aunties tied the blanket around them, as has been the custom for centuries. The crowd clapped when Paulie made a big show of poking the blanket so that everyone thought they kissed under the cover. They probably did. When Father Bob announced the couple as joined in marriage, some applauded, some let out whoops of congratulations. Big Man presented to them their marriage stick, and together as a couple, they carved the first notch into it.

The guests strolled across the street to find the buffet line back at the Cultural Center.

After helping serve the cake, she looked for a way to back out of the ongoing festivities gracefully. She didn't want to add any grist for the rumor mill. She had taken enough photos for her gift album. Excited to start on it, she doubted anyone would miss her if she silently slipped away.

Beverly Waters McBride

Chapter Twenty-Three

Maryville/Miami

Dan called from the Atlanta airport to tell Beth he was on his way to Miami for vacation. His call thrilled her, since hearing from him meant he thought about her.

"I just called to say hello." More than just tired, he sounded sad or maybe dejected.

"I'm doing fine," she reported. "I'm still waiting for the school to become aware they need to hire me after all. Where did you travel to this time?"

"I spent time in Europe, mostly Amsterdam. Now I need some time off, so I'm going to vacation in Miami for a few weeks. It's a great time of year to go there. No snow, no plowing, no coats, scarves or gloves, you know?" She again detected more emotion under the surface of his light banter.

"You sound tired. Are you OK?" she asked.

"Yeah. I just need a break."

In the time period since renewing their friendship, despite spending a little more time together, their new romance hadn't yet taken off again with any exclusivity.

Still, it touched her that he seemed to be having issues bothering him. For him to sound so depressed worried her. She didn't like the idea of his being alone, gone from his friends and family. She tried to think of anything she could do to help him.

She hadn't yet told him about her art studio by the river or her growing reputation in the art world. He'd been out of town quite a bit. Rather than keeping it from him, she liked to think they'd discuss it later, more naturally, maybe after he returned from this trip. Or better yet, maybe she ought to fly down to Miami to surprise him. She'd go to him. That's it! She'd also plan to visit one or two of the galleries exhibiting her work down there and maybe rent a car to swing over to Naples and Sanibel Island on the Gulf Coast.

She'd never done anything so impulsive, probably ever. Maybe he'd want to go with her to Sanibel. Now that sounded like fun! Maybe Melinda would tell her where he stayed in Miami.

She called Melinda to find out where he stayed in Miami, since if anyone may know, Melinda would. She nervously thumbed through the small Maryville phone book, as she waited for Melinda to answer her phone.

"Hello, Melinda, this is Beth."

"Oh. Beth," she said. "What can I do for you?"

"I'm hoping you know Dan's schedule, maybe where he might be staying in Miami. He called me last night so I'd like to get back to him," she said.

Melinda hesitated a moment, then said, "He always stays in those fancy hotels right on the beach. He says he prefers those pricy hotels everywhere he goes. Nothing but the best for my brother, the world traveler." Beth rolled her eyes. "What, you going there, too?" Melinda asked, a bit too perceptively.

Beth gulped, flushing bright red, grateful Melinda couldn't see all this over the phone, then stammered, "I thought I'd head that way. I might run into him."

"Oh, then ask him about his adventure down there. It involved the police, a mugging and to hear him tell it, he came out a hero." Melinda sounded skeptical.

"I'll ask him to tell me about it. Thanks." She hung up thinking Melinda might be on her side after all.

Anxious to move forward making her arrangements, she called the galleries she expected to visit. The gallery owners in Naples and Sanibel gushed with excitement at the prospect of her coming, immediately scheduling receptions. She looked forward to meeting people who liked her work. She expected some ego-boosting, VIP treatment, and to show off a bit for Dan, too.

The prospect of surprising Dan brought a smile to her face. She'd never seen an ocean beach, only the fresh water Great Lakes. She planned on taking some scenic photography of the area for inspiration, so she over packed, as usual, with photo gear, clothing for every conceivable occasion, sketch books, pastels, and supplies.

Upon settling in at the hotel in Miami, she immediately walked out to the beach with her shoes in her hand, to experience the cool ocean breeze, smell the salty sea air and revel in the warm sand between her toes. Bringing her hands to her tongue, she tasted the unfamiliar salty water. It tasted fishy. It even smelled different from the fresh water lakes she knew.

Shading her eyes to gaze across the water, she surmised the tiny specks off shore must be huge ocean ships. Overhead, sea birds flew, making their characteristic bird sounds. The horizon stretched endlessly as the gentle motion of the waves broke along the shoreline. The sound of the surf enchanted her, filled her ears, just as the tropical colors, pastels in blue and green lulled her into relaxing. She heaved a big sigh of relief, tension melting away with each breath, drawn to the small, ocean-side bank of swaying palm trees. They were surrounded with low, native tropical bushes, seemingly just growing out of the white sand.

Strolling along the shoreline between the expanse of beach and paved parking lots, past multi-storied luxury hotels and residential condos, she became aware of sweat on her face and body. Other people walked along in front and behind her, almost in a column, like an unengineered tourist train careening down the shore. She didn't dare stoop to pick up a shell for fear of being rear-ended. The white sand beach, littered with towels, chairs, coolers and plastic everything, accommodated walkers, sunbathers and swimmers of all ages. Children waded in the surf, squealing, playing with buckets and plastic rafts, chasing water birds.

Back at the hotel, she knocked on Dan's door, getting no answer. She wanted to surprise him, so decided to try again the next morning. Thinking he'd be pleased to see her, especially after calling her last week, she'd be able to cheer him up.

Rising early to catch the spectacular sunrise the next morning, she knocked a cheerful pattern onto his door. The door opened and there stood Dan, shirtless, hips wrapped in a fluffy white hotel towel. His head almost jerked backwards in surprise as his mind registered she stood there, outside his door.

She smiled until she recognized from his reaction, he may well be shocked to see her.

He stepped aside, inviting her in. She saw then why he acted surprised. Sitting at the table in his luxurious suite, eating breakfast, a beautiful, long-haired, olive-skinned Hispanic woman wore the smallest of string bikinis. The woman seemed to be hanging out of the thing! Her tanned body could only be described as voluptuous. A damp hotel robe hung on the back of her chair, so Beth concluded they recently enjoyed a morning swim.

"Uh, Bonnie, this is a dear friend of mine from home, Beth. Beth, this is Bonnie, uh, Detective Bonita Torque, of the Miami/Dade Police."

Beth said nothing as the shock of finding him there with another woman, registered. She recovered enough to extend her hand and say, "Hello." He allowed both women to draw their own conclusions. They looked each other over without comment. Beth did her best to remain polite and neutral.

Bonnie, the first to recover her manners, insisted Beth join them in their room service breakfast. "You must join us," she said. "We have plenty. I'd love the chance to talk to one of Dan's good friends." She asked Dan to bring over another chair.

Beth searched for any guile in her words or expression, finding none. She also tried to refuse, to make up an excuse. Having no graceful way out, she reluctantly sat on the edge of the chair as they made small talk about the good weather and the ocean.

Dan excused himself to dress.

Beth apologized to Bonnie for interrupting their meal. "I'm so sorry to barge in. I tried to reach Dan last night, but we failed to connect, so I thought I'd try again this morning."

Bonnie said, "Please, don't worry. We found ourselves hungry after an early swim. Try some of this fresh squeezed OJ," she said, nibbling on a cantaloupe square as she drank coffee. She'd covered up with the robe, which helped Beth's comfort level. Miss Bonnie certainly looked like a healthy, contented woman. It was hard not to hate her with her sterling manners and winsome ways. *I hate her! Actually, I like her. She's very nice. I still hate her!*

After offering Beth a basket of sweet rolls and pouring her a glass of orange juice, Bonnie asked, "What brings you to Miami?"

She searched for a worthy answer. "I'm going to visit some art galleries here in town and on the Gulf Coast," she explained. She doubted Bonnie believed it. Hell, she wouldn't have believed it herself. How naive of her not to expect that Dan wasn't seeing other women on his world travels? Of course, he met women. Melinda, his sister, already told her as much. As a normal, attractive guy, he'd be a perfect match for this smart, beautiful woman.

Dan came back in record time, dressed in chinos and Polo shirt. Sweating, both figuratively and literally, he made the best of a dicey situation.

"Beth tells me she's visiting art galleries in the area," Bonita said too enthusiastically. Her voice now betrayed a little sharp edge, although on the surface she kept her discomfort disguised.

Dan tilted his head, looking at Beth, as if waiting to hear her answer.

"Yes, I'll be here today and tomorrow," she said, with shallow enthusiasm. "Then the next day, I'll be driving across state to Naples, then on up the coast to Sanibel Island. I hope to see some of the countryside in the Everglades on the way, maybe look for an alligator."

"That sounds nice," she said politely.

"Bonnie, you're working tomorrow, right?" he asked.

"Yes," she said, looking at him speculatively, speaking volumes with her short response. She looked directly at Beth, her expression conveying 'keep your hands off my man,' or definitely something close to it.

He looked pointedly toward Beth, saying, "Then maybe we'll meet for brunch tomorrow to catch up. Tell me more about your gallery tour."

"Sure," she said, moving toward the door, thanking Bonnie for her hospitality and the OJ.

"I'll call you tomorrow morning after you have a chance to get your bearings, OK?" he repeated at the door. "I'm glad to see you. I look forward to seeing you again tomorrow."

She stood there a moment, incredulous. She couldn't even work up a righteous indignation that the woman was a bitch, for she was nice and polite, too. She lectured herself all the way back to her room. She wasn't going to melt away over this. She still had galleries to see, admirers to meet, and obligations to fulfill. She'd get on with her life, and make it great.

Despite previously imagining Dan escorting her to the party tonight, in reality, she could perfectly well go by herself. She opted to spend the rest of the morning finding the two galleries displaying her work here in Miami, telling them she'd arrived. She'd go back to the beach this afternoon, then come back early enough to dress for the Artist's Reception in her honor this evening. The gallery arranged to send over a limo, so she'd be content to sip champagne tonight and make witty small talk with her fans here in Miami.

She woke up the next morning with a champagne hangover—the worst kind. She hadn't acted with such abandon in a long time. She opened one eye to check the surroundings before requiring her body to move. The bedside clock read eight-thirty. Sun streamed in around the drawn drapes. She vaguely remembered wading in the ocean with her Jimmy Choo's in hand, giggling like a girl each time the waves caught the hem of her dress, trying not to spill the expensive champagne from her glass. Beyond that, the evening blurred. She became aware of fuzziness clouding up her head, punctuated with sound of rushing water far away. Then ringing assaulted her ears. No—wait, might that be the phone?

The bedside phone rang again like a bomb exploding in her head. Wincing, she grabbed it before it rang again. "Hello," her dry, husky voice rasped.

"Hi, Beth, this is Dan. First, let me apologize for the big shock yesterday. I never expected to see you standing there when I opened the door. I never want to embarrass, upset or hurt you in any way."

"Yes," she croaked out from her dry, thirsty, mouth.

"I'd like to meet you this morning, to talk to you," he said with intensity. "Meet me downstairs at nine-thirty? It's a little after eight-thirty now. You've probably been up for hours."

"No, actually I haven't …" she replied. Right then, the bathroom door opened. Out strolled a half-naked, towel-covered, gorgeous man, obviously just out of her shower. He toweled wet hair as he walked toward her. She stared at him, almost dropping the phone.

Paralyzed, she swallowed, reclutching the phone. A strange man didn't stroll out of her bathroom every day. He held her full attention.

"Good morning," he said in her direction.

"Good morning," she muttered, covering the receiver. "Dan, can we make it closer to ten o'clock?" she choked out, watching the man walking around her room. He knew she watched him, too. He preened a little for her benefit.

"Sure, ten o'clock it is, in the restaurant downstairs. They boast a great breakfast buffet here, by the way. See ya' then!" Thankfully, he hung up.

She had other fish to fry right now. She could only handle one gorgeous hunk of man at a time. She didn't know this handsome devil very well—in fact, she didn't remember him at all. He, on the other hand, seemed quite at home here and acted unfazed by anything, such as a potentially regretful female with a messed-up memory. She wanted to remember him all right, with his fabulous tan, meaty biceps and fine, chiseled facial features. His sun-bleached, blond hair, with long sideburns looked just the least bit wild.

Now that he wore a bit more, at least with pants on, she could think. He sat down on the edge of the bed, putting on his socks. Those massive, well-toned shoulders, rippling with each movement he made, distracted her momentarily, slowly remembering him—the limo driver from last night.

"You survived—slightly wasted last night," he remarked as leaned over, kissing her on the forehead. "You sure liked the champagne."

She checked her body, lifting the all-covering bed sheet, taking hope since she still wore her underwear. She clutched the sheet up to her neck.

"I don't remember much," she admitted. "You're …," she searched her mind for his name, "… Tim. Did we… ?" she asked, tentatively.

"No darlin'. There are still some good guys left in Miami." He pointed to the couch where he'd left a blanket and pillow.

"I tricked you back to your room by promising you a 'good time', before you conked out completely. I wanted to be sure you arrived here safely. Don't worry, it's an occupational hazard for me. I don't mind, especially when the customers are as nice and fun as you. You're a great drunk, too. Some people become mean, others messy, whereas, you just grew funnier, more carefree. We didn't do anything to worry about, young lady, other than some first-class kissing. I try not to extract any advantage of my drunken customers. It's better for everyone that way."

He walked over to his shoes, then sat in the chair looking at her. Relief flooded her body. He seemed like a really nice guy. His business card lay on the table beside the bed. Tim's Limos. He owned the limo company.

"I'm going to head out now. If you need another ride while you're here, call me, OK?"

"Wait, Tim," she said, as she jumped out of bed, stumbling over the huge sheet wrapped around her, then catching herself. "Give me a sec." She rummaged through her bag in the top dresser drawer, taking out some cash to give him. He raised his hand in protest.

"Look, you didn't have to be so nice, you had the opportunity to rob me, or worse. I appreciate your taking care of me instead. Please accept this." She held out some cash.

He shrugged, then turned away and looking back, saluted her goodbye, as he shut the door. She just stood there for a moment, still clutching the bills, not believing her good luck to find a decent person to help her when she had made some clearly questionable choices.

As the warm shower cascaded over her throbbing head and body, she tried to think it through. In the cold light of day, she couldn't believe she'd engaged in such dangerous behavior! At least, she was only embarrassed this morning. She'd not done anything akin to getting so blitzed in years. Directed inward, she fumed, until she comprehended all this anger unreasonably centered on Dan. As she dressed, eventually it hit her that Dan hadn't poured the champagne down her throat. She chose this behavior for herself. Yes, he called her a few days ago. However, her mistake became inserting herself into his vacation, uninvited.

She arrived downstairs early to meet Dan in the lobby. They made their way to the hotel's elaborate dining room, opting for the breakfast buffet, complete with omelets to order and waffle chefs creating your choices on demand. They sat at one of several tables-for-two lining a huge picture window that framed a panoramic view of Miami Beach. Already mid-morning, tourists dotted the sand, jockeying for a better position to catch the unrelenting sunshine.

Talk at their table, inconsequential at first, centered on exchanging opinions about the local weather, and then exhausting that topic, catching up on every Yooper's favorite subject—winter, differences in the weather, and coping skills up north. The second most favored topic, 'Who are your relatives,' they already knew, so no need to drone on over that one.

They ate the buffet brunch, at least he ate, since breakfast foods were not her first choice this morning, and they drank the strong coffee. He asked about her education experiences and artistic life.

"So tell me about visiting art galleries here. What's up with that?" he asked. She narrowed her eyes, pondering whether to big deal it, hitting him between the eyes with her information, or to ease into sharing with him.

"I finally finished my MFA in fine arts," she said shyly. "You knew I attended some college courses in Maryville over the years. I finished up at American University while I lived in Maryland. After that, I worked at a small art gallery for a while, and still have a financial interest in it, so I stay on top of the art business. We feature the work of native artists from Africa. It's been a real springboard for my own work as well." She shared more about her successes, about her current studio in Maryville. He stared at her, taking it all in. It made her happy to finally share with him.

"I congratulate you for your accomplishments," he said, clinking coffee mugs. "I'm very impressed with all you've done, Beth. I had no idea, but I like hearing you found your passion, especially in the midst of all the personal drama going on as well."

"Thanks. I wanted to tell you for a while but I don't like to brag. I'd rather you see my stuff, then judge for yourself."

"I knew you had skills, I knew you had it in there," he said, as he touched his finger to her forehead then lowered his finger to her heart, his eyes never leaving hers. Raw emotions swept her body. She found the gesture mesmerizing, and erotic, much different from when her professor at AU made a similar gesture. She blinked, brushed his hand away, holding it in hers for a while, in the intimacy of the moment. She shuddered involuntarily, allowing him his hand back.

"Your appreciation means a lot to me, Dan. You know that."

"I know you've been through some changes. I hope you know I want to be there for you. I want to be in your life, now and in the future," he added.

They sat just looking at one another, without speaking. They each plumbed the depths behind the other's dark eyes, in the way of comfortable lovers. Beth held her breath, wanting to draw out the intensity of the moment.

He broke it, taking another swig of his coffee, and said, "I'm only human," as if in apology.

"Speaking of humanity," she said. "I want to tell you I like Bonnie. She seems like a great person. Maybe I'm crazy to admit it. She came across as a kind person, even in the awkwardness of our meeting. How long have you known her, how did you meet?"

"We met when I got mugged here in Miami a while back. She didn't think a lot of me at first. I came here on business and just happened to be in the wrong place, wrong time, on the beach. For about thirty seconds I survived as a mugging victim, until I conquered my assailants. Then the good detective questioned me about the reports from the perps at the ER about a "demon" attacking them on the beach. Nothing said by them, of course, about their taking my keys and wallet before I whomped them. Then, later in the same day, back at my hotel, I helped a lady in distress. She just happened to be involved in a domestic thing. I couldn't just stand by watching. I didn't have my ID back yet, so the local LEO's called Bonnie because of the earlier case and we encountered each other again." He laughed. "She found it rare to run into the same tourist two times in one day, so we went for drinks. I've come back to see her a time or two since then."

Beth found this story amusing. She remembered Melinda's suggestion to ask him about his exploits with the police in Miami. A gifted tease and story embroiderer, even if it unfolded as he said, she knew she ought to look twice before swallowing the whole story. It made a good yarn, though.

He watched her reaction, then said seriously, "Bonnie is a good friend. She's smart and fun to be with. Her heart and soul live here in this community. She's tied to this town, her job, her culture and family, just as you and I are to ours in the UP. We might go away for a while, but the pull to go home is irresistible."

Beth nodded in understanding. Their eyes locked. He silently reaffirmed that Bonnie didn't pose a threat to her relationship with him. He told her without words that his capacity to appreciate Bonnie's needs, without pushing her away out of jealousy or fear, actually showed he had matured over the years, had grown from the old insecure, arrogant Dan. She liked that. No longer a child, he allowed another's interests ahead of his own, which meant there might perhaps be hope for the two of them, also. If he showed that sort of generosity of spirit, perhaps their own relationship could rise to a greater spiritual level, too, given time.

They hugged and kissed in parting, she ready for her trip to Naples, he to attend to whatever he planned for the day. Reluctant to make plans for her return, not knowing for sure when she'd be back, they hadn't discussed getting back together. Besides, she wanted to give Dan his vacation time, even if it meant sharing him with Bonnie. She could give him that gift for now.

Chapter Twenty-Four

Naples/Sanibel Island

She loved Sanibel Island. Her heart warmed as she drove across the causeway from the mainland to the unique resort island. People long ago recognized the exceptional beauty of the trip or why else would anyone pay such a huge bridge toll? She contrasted taking the Sugar Island ferry across the river channel in Maryville to Sugar Island—similar feelings, conquerable cost.

When the toll tender gave her a cheerful "Six dollars, please," she didn't even blink.

She forked over the cash, adding an equally cheerful "Thank you," in return.

The blue-green hue of the Gulf water, gentle lapping of the waves on the shore, and swaying palms in the chamber of commerce-endorsed sunny weather gave her a visceral appreciation of the contrasts of this exotic location.

Sanibel, the island, teemed with residents having a bipolar love/hate affection for old Florida natural charm, juxtaposed with sporadic avant-garde architecture. They also maintained an enduring fascination with the arts. She enjoyed the contrast, a shanty fishing shack abutting a modern boutique shopping mall.

Cool breezes off the Gulf rustled the huge Australian Pines and palm tree fronds in an almost musical sound. Islands of dark green, tall trees sat in sandy, low, natural vegetation clusters along the narrow streets. The roads, many unpaved, dead ended into beach or bay hotels, condos, marinas or boat docks. The vehicle traffic choked the roads, while one, two and three-wheeled bicycles hazarded the sidewalks, along with pedestrians and strollers everywhere.

The clerk at her hotel recommended dining at the Bubble Room, and not to miss driving through the Ding Darling Sanctuary near sundown when the birds and wildlife come out to dazzle onlookers armed only with binoculars and cameras. She also wanted to view the Bailey's two-level grocery store, select groceries that travel down a conveyer belt to the first floor for loading into her car, which sure sounded fun to watch.

In the late afternoon traffic, the first two times she drove around the block she missed the Mayer Gallery building. Made of cypress wood, tucked off the thoroughfare in a discrete boutique area, eventually she found it. Sasha Mayer, the gallery owner, greeted her graciously, assuring her that all the people invited to meet her at the reception tonight were friendly and appreciative.

"These people love art," he said. "They will be delighted to meet you."

It surprised her to find a crowd of well-wishers already mingling. Others kept arriving throughout the evening. They munched on wine, cheese, and cute little hors d'oeuvres. They asked questions and actually listened to her answers. As a person not having been listened to or heard for most of her life, when people listened to her now about art, her safety subject, she soared.

"What are you working on now?" asked one particularly inquisitive fellow. He focused on her intently, looking as if he lived for her response.

She replied thoughtfully, "I'm appreciating the pastels and sunset colors of Florida right now. There's lightness about natural subjects and the unique sunlight reflected here. I may want to build a series on those subjects. You don't expect me to repeat the same thing over and over, do you?" she asked, touching his arm as if asking for indulgence. He melted for her. "You understand I'd want to grow and evolve, eh?" she asked, blinking her eyes in flirtation.

He nodded, impressed. "But it's the bold and bright colors of your work that we love so much now," he interjected. Others gathered around, nodding and agreeing. "I'm buying this beautiful yellow buttercup piece tonight, if Sasha will agree to let it go. I've been eyeing it for a while now, and since we've met, I want it even more."

"Anything for a price?" Sasha retorted.

"Just promise you'll send us some of your new work, too, won't you?"

"I'll make a special effort to send you some new ideas this year. Are you a fan of my pottery as well?" she asked, maneuvering her adoring fan expertly to the wine fountain for a refill. As they went, she laid the groundwork for selling some pieces she already had in mind with a Florida motif.

So her excursion to the Gulf Coast turned out successful—not only financially—her soul had been fed a little, too.

Chapter Twenty-Five
Miami

After she returned to Miami from her whirlwind tour to Naples and Sanibel Island, she found herself at loose ends for a day or two before her return flight with nothing particular planned. She decided to try her hand at sketching a few Floridascapes. She headed to the beach carrying her fold up chair, cooler of Pepsi, bottled water, big hat, flip flops, beach towel, sun tan lotion, novel, sun glasses, art supplies, iPod, camera, cell phone and big beach umbrella. At the last minute, she'd tucked the limo guy's business card into her beach bag. Self-consciously, she thought she probably looked ridiculous trying to balance all that gear trekking along the beach in the sand to find her perfect spot.

Settling on the sand, she staked out her site with a huge towel, placed the umbrella upright for shade and rubbed her body down with sunscreen, then drew a few rough sketches. She stared out into the gentle green hued ocean waves along the shoreline. Tiring, she read a few pages of her novel, then restless, searched her stuff for Tim's card. She'd been grateful to him after their little encounter, realizing responsible people didn't behave so recklessly. The prospects of all the things that might well have happened under those circumstances boggled her mind. Somehow she trusted Tim, even in her foggy, diminished state. He proved to be a good, honest, reliable person. She dialed his number.

"Hi Tim, this is Beth from a few nights ago. Remember me?"

"Yes, I remember. It's nice to hear from you again. Feeling better?"

"Well, I have some free time, so thought I'd ask if you'd like to join me for lunch or drinks in the next few days. I'd like to hear more about your occupational hazards."

"That might be fun. See, if you're nice to people, it comes back to you. Why don't I pick you up tonight and we'll find dinner. The limos are covered by other drivers tonight, so I'm free. Well, not exactly free, but inexpensive," he joked. They agreed to meet in the hotel lobby.

She dressed casual for the evening, choosing a designer sundress with a matching shawl, from her newly acquired Miami wardrobe, with a big, campy, bead necklace, jangling bangle bracelets, chandelier earrings. High-heeled sandals

Up the Creek

completed the look. She admired her outfit in the mirror beside the hotel elevator. Ready early, she waited in the hotel lobby for him to arrive.

She spotted him immediately when he entered the hotel. He wore a tailored sport jacket over a floral 'Miami' print shirt. He smelled divine, greeted her with a kiss on the neck, right under her ear, giving her shivers.

"I thought you'd like to try a local restaurant out on the causeway," he said.

"Yes, I could go for some fresh seafood," she said, concurring with his choice.

"This restaurant has steak, seafood, and a wonderful Caesar salad they make right at your table. Shall we go?"

They strolled to his car, still parked in the hotel driveway, a sleek, shiny, dark convertible with the top down. As they walked, his hand floated gently between her shoulder blades, a warm, light touch in a gesture of familiarity.

"Is the wind too much? Usually, with the heat here, driving at night with the top down is my one relief."

"No, it's great. I love to see the whole sky overhead and feel the wind around us, like we're in a little moving bubble, you know? You own some great CDs to pick from, too." He reached across her to the glove box, pulled out a jam-packed CD box, then spread it out for her. "I like many different kinds of music. I usually just plug in my iPod, but tonight, its ladies choice, so you select us some good tunes." She leafed through disc after disc of his impressive eclectic collection, settling back comfortably with some easy listening saxophone as they made small talk along the way.

He parked on a dark side street. They strolled to a non-descript building with no outside signage. Momentary uneasy, it dawned on her how many unknowns faced her in this situation, like strange man, strange city, strange neighborhood. She decided to be exhilarated, taking a chance, trusting Tim yet again.

Behind the dark glass doors etched with lobsters and shrimp, they entered a busy, upscale restaurant with nautical theme décor, with hanging nets and cork floats. It looked nice inside, with elegant tablecloths, matching napkins and no ketchup bottles growing bacteria left out on tables. Low-hung lighting and glass partitions stretched between booths created a modicum of privacy between tables.

The tasseled menu held pages of choices, everything prepared to order. On Tim's recommendation she opted for the Caesar salad, and enjoyed seeing it prepared before them by the waiter. They also indulged in a mound of peel-and-eat shrimp for appetizers.

"I hope I don't embarrass you by eating so many of these fabulous shrimp," she asked hesitatingly.

"On the contrary," he said. "It's good to see a woman with a healthy appetite enjoying her food. Go right ahead—just leave some room for dessert." He winked.

After their meal, he insisted they at least split the restaurant's signature dessert, a perfectly prepared flan, and a café cubano. She agreed to a café con leche instead, strong coffee with cream. They sat enjoying the coffee in companionable silence, relaxed and comfortable.

After dinner, they went to South Beach to see the night's action. Miami's unique night scene, known for young people dancing in the streets, offered a distinctly Latin sound, loud, with no apology. The people they met looked as if they had just stepped out of the pages of a fashion magazine. Tim greeted many of them introducing Beth, although the noise level prevented any meaningful conversation. These beautiful people also specialized in wearing as little as possible, as tight as possible.

Tim surprised her by being a great dancer, too. He knew and obviously socialized with many of these people. They danced on the edge of the crowd. He taught her some sizzling salsa moves. She enjoyed learning and remembering the steps, showed off just a little. She saw some of the other women looking at him with smoldering expressions, so considered herself lucky to enjoy him as her escort this evening. Attentive to her alone, he looked oblivious of the other women around them. It was great for her ego.

Romance fluttered on the air or at least made some hefty promises in the dark, warm night. Cooling breeze and picture postcard moonlight reflected on the water.

Later they walked along the beach again, arm in arm, sand squishing under her feet. Stealing kisses as the waves lapped the shore, the big, bright moon and stars twinkled overhead. Even the salty sea breeze flowed around them, wrapping them in a lover's cocoon.

She woke up the next morning, stretching under the soft white sheets in her hotel room. She looked over at the chair, saw Tim's clothing hanging there and heard the shower running. This time, he'd been invited to stay. This time she grinned, listening to the water from the shower, imagining him, real and powerful with water running all around him. Realizing although she liked Tim, a down side remained like a giant elephant in the living room. The great geographical distance between them loomed. Fireworks, while nice in a relationship, don't compare with safe, comfortable, and accessible, like with Dan.

Tim came out of the shower, hair wet and towel wrapped around his narrow hips. He leaned over to give her a sizzling kiss. A knock on the door made them both laugh.

"Please, you catch it, I'm kinda unpresentable," she asked, covering her grinning mouth.

"Sure," he said, toweling off his hair and stepping into jeans. He opened the door to a shocked Dan Walkin standing in the hallway.

"Uh, I'm looking for Beth," he stammered.

"May I tell her who's asking?" Tim asked proprietarily. He gave Dan an assessing look.

"Please tell her it's Dan."

Beth cringed, now the shoe emerged on the other foot. It pinched.

Sheet wrapped, graceful as manageable under the circumstances, she introduced Tim to Dan. Tim tactfully grabbed his other clothes then retreated to the bathroom to dress, leaving them to more private conversation.

"You made some new friends here, too," Dan teased.

"Yes," she managed to croak. "You heard I made it back from the Gulf Coast?"

"Yes, I checked downstairs. I'd like to see some of your work, if you'll let me see it. Maybe this afternoon? That is, unless you're already booked," he said with a tilt of his head toward the bathroom.

"Can I get back to you a little later? We need to decide our plans. Since I'll be leaving tomorrow, I want to tie up loose ends today, you know?"

"I understand. Do you want to pass on this afternoon, maybe touch base later?" he offered, without emotion, giving her every polite option.

"Let me see what's going to unfold here. I'll call you later this morning."

"Sure. I'll wait to hear from you," he smiled at her. With a twinkle in his eye, he said "I think you're healing just fine, don't you?"

She grinned, shutting the door without comment, but wishing he might at least have sounded a little jealous.

She flopped into a heap on the bed, covering her head, too. She heard Tim come out of the bathroom. He walked over to her, wrapping her in his arms with a big, supportive hug.

"I presume that is 'the' Dan I heard all about?"

She covered her face with her hands and nodded. He crouched to his knees beside the bed, he reached for her hands, seeking her eyes. "Look, I think you're great. I'd love to see more of you. Are you moving to Miami anytime soon?"

She nodded, no, her head slowly moving side-to-side.

"I'm damn sure not moving to Northern Michigan, so we're going to be great friends with benefits, I hope, who enjoy the heck out of our time together, right?"

She looked at him, blinking, feeling regretful and relieved at the same time. How refreshing for him to let her off the hook like this.

"I'm gonna mosey along. You have my number. You know I'd love to see you again when you travel this way. Call me."

He kissed her lightly on the lips, again on the forehead and then gave her a jaunty salute, closing the door behind him.

She sighed, realizing anew what a nice guy he happened to be—no pressure, no games, uncomplicated, mature. She already learned a lot from him.

She called Dan later, making plans with him to visit one of the galleries displaying her work that afternoon. She finally shared that side of herself with him. It felt good to share experiences with him away from Maryville.

She couldn't regret coming here at all, despite her initial reservation and all that transpired. She had met Tim, but also scored big PR dividends in the galleries. She took back new impressions of the lively colors, sounds and tastes, as well as other warm memories. All in all, a good experience.

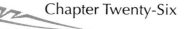

Chapter Twenty-Six

Maryville: A New Beginning

Thank goodness, she'd recently sent off several shipments of work to the D.C. gallery and to her fans in Florida. She'd worked hard the last few months to replenish their displays. Shelves storing work in her studio currently looked fairly empty. Very little stored paint and clay supplies cluttered the room.

She arrived at her workshop one morning to find that someone had broken into her studio by the river, damaged her canvasses, and emptied paint cans all over the floor. They had also broken pottery stored there from various stages of the firing process. They'd slashed her comfortable furniture and stolen her state of the art CD system. Her insurance paid for replacing the supplies and even for the expensive clean up, new furniture and electronics. She reacted more to the broken and slashed art, which could not be replaced. She contended, too, with her sense of being violated.

Who cared enough about her little enterprise to vandalize her sanctuary? The police thought it was a personal attack, asking her to think about enemies or anyone who wished her harm. She thought of no one who had it in for her or that she crossed, except maybe Marc, her ex. However, she didn't think him capable of working up this kind of angry response toward her anymore. No one else expressed feeling cheated by her or angry enough with her to go to this extreme. As instructed, while she worked to clean up the mess, she thought back over her life, imagining anything or anyone whom might be considered a suspect.

Fingerprint dust showed up all over. Paint clean up alone was a huge job, but worse, she hated seeing the waste of supplies.

Picking out new paint colors and all new furniture may be fun though. Newly fond of the sunset colors, like those Florida sunsets, the possibility of ordering some new paint supplies brought a little smile to her weary, paint-smeared face.

She decided to work first on replacing the pottery destroyed in the break in and not to spend any more time thinking about some sinister motive. Less easily replaced, the bigger loss revolved around her sentimental attachment to larger canvas art pieces stored there. It offended her artist's sensitivity that her work got trashed, although now she had an excuse to work on some new paintings.

She absently picked up her jingling cell phone. "Hi, Beth, This is Mrs. Fauls from Maryville Schools. We hope you are still available, as there is a sudden, unexpected opening in the art dept. It's for a sub position right now, until the end of the year. However, it will very likely be turned into a full-time position. We'd like you to come in as soon as possible to talk about it."

"Yes, I'd love to talk to you about it, but I'm kind of in the middle of something today, could I come tomorrow?" she said as she looked around her wrecked studio, paint everywhere, her clothes saturated in the pungent smell of solvent for the oils and water for the acrylics. Paint covered her hands and face. For this opportunity, though, she'd stop the cleanup and go to the school board.

"Tomorrow is fine. Come early, about nine o'clock, and we'll sign forms. See you then."

First, Beth sighed in resignation that her clean up would be delayed. But she needed this boost right now, in the midst of all this chaos. It would be the beginning of accomplishing her long-held dreams.

She went to see Mrs. Fauls at the School Board, signing all the necessary papers. She planned to start the next Monday. She already knew she'd love watching her students opening up artistically, like spring flowers.

Beth stepped in for the last two months of the year, challenging and praising students. She became busy arranging the end-of-year showings at each elementary and middle school. She helped them complete their end-of-year projects. Displaying their work and inviting parents and family to view their efforts added to the excitement for them and her. She saw a difference in the work the students produced in just a few months, compared to the prior seven months of the school year under Barry Warren. She believed the students and their parents could see it, too.

"A fellow by the name of Alfred Milton, AKA Barry Warren broke into your studio and trashed it, Ms. Morrison," the Police Officer McClennan told her, leafing through his notebook. "He left town right after he got fired from the school board. That happened the day of your break in. He's evidently tried since then to establish himself in Ohio. We received a call from the Cincinnati PD. They're questioning him. That's about all we know for now." So that explained the sudden opening in the schools that no one wanted to talk about. Barry had been fired, according to the officer. She had been hired to fill his spot.

"Thanks for the information, officer. Do you suspect he'll be back this way, should I worry?"

"Don't worry. You may take the precaution of locking your door, as you probably should anyway, right?"

She nodded, trying to imagine why the person she knew as Barry would do that kind of damage to her, why he wanted to break in or destroy her work. Unresolved questions popped into her head.

She spared a few minutes to speculate over Barry Warren, since their brief meeting at Wal-Mart showed clearly that their philosophies differed. Yes, they disagreed about teaching philosophy, but it hadn't been so terrible, she thought. She hadn't confronted him. She hardly knew him. She wondered how he even knew about the studio, unless he had followed her here sometime.

Some little something about him nagged at her. In a way, his misfortune helped her, since she'd finally been given her opportunity. She looked forward to beginning the next year, having the whole year to work with the kids. She focused more on her plans for the future, rather than dwelling on the past.

Beverly Waters McBride

Chapter Twenty-Seven

Maryville: Retribution

Tired, but working late at her studio one Friday night, she still had the urge to work at something creative, to focus her energy. After finishing a busy week at school, she was getting to know her students and coming up with a routine. She quit the casino after her school job came through. Now she could complete her martial arts workout each night, then hit her studio for some personal creative time. She looked forward to getting her hands dirty and her paintbrushes wet on her own projects.

She pondered calling her friend, Marty, to meet her for lunch on Saturday. As usual, she had the music playing pretty loud, blocking out any other distractions. She liked the scent of the spring air, slightly damp, wafting in through the open door and the lingering coolness. She frequently left the rolling garage door open in the evenings, feeling safe here, even after the previous break-in.

She concentrated on mixing the new paints for the precise color she intended to adorn the canvas in front of her.

Only a second before he attacked had she any inkling someone lurked behind her.

Suddenly, he grabbed her roughly around the neck, pulling her up tight against him with one arm while a huge sharp knife blade, long, shiny silver, gleamed before her eyes. Startled as much as afraid, she froze.

"I've got you now, bitch," a tight voice spoke roughly into her ear, pulling the knife even closer toward her. Now, her fear surfaced. While her instinct dictated she flip and disarm him, first she wanted to first find out what this was about. Her martial arts training gave her the confidence that she could deal with him before he did her any real harm. She maintained control of the situation, despite the drama of it.

"What's this about?" she asked, careful not to fight him or betray herself as capable of disarming him at any moment. She'd rather try to talk him down first.

"You, bitch, that's what this is about. You've taken my job now, my career. You turned them all against me, again. You think I don't know you planned this, planned taking everything away from me, even in school back in D.C. right up to now? I came here to be where you lived before and then you came back

Up the Creek

here to capture everything away, just like you did with that husband of yours. You come in and mess everything up!" He whined plaintively, pulling her even tighter around the neck. Any tighter, she might lose consciousness.

"Look, Barry, I didn't mean to mess anything up for you. I don't remember meeting you before coming here."

That proved evidently the wrong tack. He turned redder with rage. "I know that, you controlling bitch! You never even saw me. You looked right through me and only had eyes for 'Professor Dreamy,'" he mocked. "We sat right in class together and you never even looked my way. All the teachers fawned over your paintings, but never said a word to me."

"I'm sorry, Barry. I didn't remember you went to school with me." Then it dawned on her that he was the student snubbed by Professor Dreamy, the one who dropped out after that incident. "You look completely different. I didn't recognize you. I would never knowingly insult or undermine you. I happened to be pretty wrapped up in my own troubles at the time. I don't want to hurt you or anyone else, ever."

"Well you did. You took everything from me. I've been following behind you ever since. I found all about your precious gallery in Georgetown. They found that little fire I started there before any damage could be done, dammit. And your secret studio here in this warehouse, I'll bet you had fun after I left here the last time. I made a huge mess for you to clean up. You have everything—it just falls into your lap. I have nothing and can't get anything. Well, it changes now, you stupid, stupid, bitch, somebody's going to pay for all that's been done to me and you're elected."

With that, he raised the knife tightly against her throat.

It happened fast. She went into survival mode, no longer thinking at all, elbowed him in the solar plexus, grabbed his head then laid him out on the floor. He lay still. She kicked the knife out of reach and turned him over to bind his hands. She grabbed some electrical tape, trussing him up like a turkey. She found her cell and called the police.

Once the city police arrived, car after car came to the scene, lights flashing in the dark night. Officers of all kinds, from city, tribal, fish and game and even some Coast Guard guys stood around talking, surveying the scene and walking with clipboards, all looking terribly efficient.

One of the last to arrive, Dan's car came rushing in, skidding to a stop in front of her. He jumped out, door ajar, and came straight to her, pushing the others aside, hugging her for dear life.

"Oh, my gosh, are you okay?" he whispered in her ear. He also planted a big kiss on her lips, just in case any of the other guys didn't get it yet that she already had admirers.

"Yes, I'm fine, thank you," she said clearly, while allowing him to hold her close for a while, anyway. It felt safe and warm.

"Whoa, slugger, watch out for this lady," one of the guys nearby offered. "She's got skills." He teased, despite the humorless smirk sent his way from an unamused Dan. The officer let out a big guffaw, and poked a nearby colleague. They chuckled, then both walked away, shaking their heads, to huddle with their police cronies.

Dan tenderly cradled Beth's head, pressing her to his shoulder. He'd speak to the boys about that comment later.

Barry, or Alfred, sat cuffed in the back of the police car. They'd released him from the duct tape binding, cuffed him and loaded him into the back of the car for safekeeping. Practically the whole force came out for this arrest, since a fugitive had been captured by a civilian, a female to boot.

Beth became the hero of the hour. Everyone around the scene spoke in hushed tones about how she'd disarmed and subdued her attacker, all without sustaining a scratch. Barry/Alfred still screamed invectives at her, from the back of the police car, although no one listened to him. He sounded hoarse now.

Officer McClennen summed up the situation for all of them, but mostly for Dan's benefit at this point. "This perp is wanted both in D.C. and Wisconsin for assaults and frauds. He stole the identity of a Barry Warren, and Mr. Warren is missing. He's wanted for questioning about that. He stole Warren's teaching credentials. That's how he obtained his job here. At least, he's never gonna be exposed to innocent children again, I hope. He'll get some time for this assault, maybe kidnapping, fraud, falsehood under oath and identity theft, if not worse, once the investigation is complete." McClennen looked smug.

"I won't ask how you executed it," Dan whispered to her, "I'm just grateful you're okay.'

"You never asked me, Dan, but I'm a brown belt now. I've been working on it for a while, over at the dojo with Master Green." She snuggled closer to him. Standing here in Dan's arms made her mild interest in Master Green pale in comparison. This seemed very right, very comforting. Strong, supportive, and warm, he showed he cared about her. She breathed in his spicy masculine scent.

He held her at arm's length, searching her face for something, as his own expression reflected awe over all he heard.

"Amazing," he said. "Just amazing." He hugged her to him again, wrapping his arms around her, enveloping her like a cocoon of safety, while the other guys rolled their eyes at them. He didn't care. He couldn't imagine losing her, especially now.

I guess I'll have to watch my step around you from now on," he teased, "since you are able deck me."

"Like I'm gonna do that," she retorted. "But, yeah, you better watch your p's and q's."

"I'm very proud of you for learning protective skills. Times like this show why it's good for you." He paused. "So you're the student Master Green is so proud of, the one he wanted to get to know better." She grinned primly, saying nothing.

"I'll macho up and declare my territory," he said, only half-joking.

"Will you, Dan? Am I your territory now? What about Bonnie?"

He shrugged, dishing back to her, "What about Tim?"

She shrugged this time. "You're not going back to Miami anytime soon, are you?" she asked him seriously. He walked her inside the building, out of vision and earshot of the activity outside. He pulled her to him possessively, then kissed her until she felt weak, clinging to him.

"Not if I have a reason to stay here," he said, his eyes smoldering and yearning in his expression.

Glossary of Terms

Anishnabe, Anishnabek: The Anishnabe are a family of indigenous people who historically lived along the Eastern Coast, then a Great Migration brought the people toward the Upper Great Lakes region, including Canada; the culture, discovered through language; the language.

Bamidzowin: Way of life; knowing what it is to be Anishnabe; philosophy and principles based on beliefs, belonging and connectedness; understanding is the key to the process of engaging one's self in the practicing or doing of Anishnabe.

Binnojin, Binnojii: Children, babies; the early stages of the circle of life.

Ceremony: How things are done; the Spirit is always present.

Gzheminidoo: Creator

Miigwech: Thank you.

Pow-Wow: A gathering together for relatives and community; homecoming; a time to refresh, touch base with roots, dance, drum, sing, pray, honor and celebrate.

Primatiziwin: Your personal life journey.

The People: The term of respect for native people....

Shaman: A spiritual leader; one devoted to spiritual purpose.

Tied in the blanket: A symbolic joining of the couple at wedding ceremony, symbolic of one blanket, one lodge, one home.

Tobacco: A sacred medicine, one of the four medicines; used in prayer, ceremony for a sacred purpose.

The Seven Grandfathers: Guiding principles:

> Wisdom "Nbwaakaawin";
> Love "Zaagidwin",
> Respect "Minaadendmowin",
> Bravery "Askdenhewin",
> Truth "Debwewin",
> Humility "Dbaademidizwin",
> Honesty "Gweyakwaadziwn".

Wedding stick: A tree branch, often decorated with feathers and beads given to the bride on which the newly married couple carves notches to symbolically represent good times they have together in their marriage. They are told to hang it in their bedroom, so in bad times, they can take it down, touch each notch, remembering better times. If the stick is broken, they are divorced. If she puts the stick outside the lodge, he must consult the elders before going back in.

One Foot in Two Canoes Series

Book One - **One Foot in Two Canoes**: The focus character in this book is Dan Walkin, a modern Native American man who travels the world working for the rich, powerful and famous, and then returns to his roots on the reservation. (released April 2009)

Book Two - **Up the Creek**: Second in the series about modern life as Native Americans living in the UP. Beth is the focus character. Her story is one of surviving abuse and recovery from victimization. She is Dan's childhood sweetheart. (Release March 2011)

Book Three - (working title) **Without a Paddle**: The Story of Paulie, a young man, trying to find his place in the world. He marries Luvenia, the Sheriff's daughter. This story centers on development of cultural identity.

Book Four - (working title) **Getting Wet Feet**: Dr. Lee is an Indian Health Service Pediatrician working in the town of Maryville for the Tribe. She is Navaho herself, and has lived and worked with the Chippewa Tribe for 20 years, raising her family and becoming involved in the community. Dr. Lee's story is about sacrifice, knowledge and personal responsibility.

Book Five - (working title) **Up to the Neck**: Melinda is Dan's twin sister, married to his former partner, Harry, a tribal cop. They have three kids and lots of opportunities to live their culture. Her story is about service to community, kindness and sharing, which are important Native American values.

Book Six - (working title) **Float, Swim or Drown**: Micha is a young Shaman in training, learning his lessons. His story is about developing spirituality, learning his place in his tribe and community, and living up to expectations.

Book Seven - (working title) **Rocking the Boat**: Big Man is the shaman, mentor and interpreter of community for many people searching for their identities. The life of a spiritual leader is sometimes unexpected.

LaVergne, TN USA
20 March 2011
220833LV00002B/4/P